The Place of Lions

The Place of Lions

Eric Campbell

HBJ

HARCOURT BRACE JOVANOVICH, PUBLISHERS

San Diego   New York   London

First published 1990 by Macmillan Children's Books London,
a division of Macmillan Publishers Limited.

Library of Congress Cataloging-in-Publication Data
Campbell, Eric.
The place of lions/Eric Campbell. — 1st American ed.
p.   cm.
Summary: When the plane flying Chris and his father
crashes on the Serengeti Plain, Chris sets out to find help and
finds that his journey is paralleled by that of an aging lion.
ISBN 0-15-262408-2
[1. Serengeti Plain (Tanzania) — Fiction.   2. Lions — Tanzania —
Fiction.   3. Survival — Fiction.   4. Aeronautics — Accidents —
Fiction.]   I. Title.
PZ7.C15098P1   1991
[Fic] — dc20   91-8037

Designed by Trina Stahl

First United States edition

A B C D E

The
Place of
Lions

Chapter 1

CHRIS HARRIS'S MOTHER HAD DIED WHEN HE WAS twelve. It was this devastating event, everyone agreed, that had made Chris seem so much older than his years. Unbearable though his own loss had been, he'd had to grow up overnight to help his father deal with the desolation of his grief. He'd had to, as they say, be a man.

He wasn't exactly a misfit at school, though mostly he was alone. He didn't want to play games, had no interest in soccer or the latest chart entries, and found the conversation and company of his class-mates trivial and childish. His teachers wrote strange things in his school reports about "nonparticipation in ongoing peer-group situations," which he didn't understand and suspected they didn't either. They certainly didn't understand him, that was for sure.

The truth was he'd outgrown school. He'd had enough of sitting and listening. He wanted to *do*. Just what it was he wanted to do, he wasn't exactly sure. But he had to do something. Something had to happen.

Well, something had happened. On that very day his father had delivered a piece of news that made Chris play truant for the first time in his previously law-abiding life.

The news had come at breakfast time. Just as Mr. Harris was leaving for work, he'd dropped a large brown envelope nonchalantly onto the table.

"Take a look at that, will you," he'd said. "See what you think. We can talk about it tonight."

Then, with a wink to his son, he had left, an intriguingly self-satisfied smile on his face.

The contents of the envelope had been as explosive as a hand grenade, and by the time Chris reached school his head was a fireworks display of excitement. A period of math and a period of history passed without his hearing a word, as great rocket bursts of realization and imagination fired in arcs through his mind. By break, he decided there was no point in his being there at all, so he slipped away down the back staircase to make his escape.

Turning the corner of the building, he tiptoed past the boiler room where his friend Henry, the janitor, slept for much of the day, and started across the yard toward the small wooden doorway to freedom.

That day, Henry wasn't asleep.

"First time I've seen you at this game. Them hard-knocks, Eddington and them idiots with the ear-rings—yes. They're down this way every day. Regular as Big Ben. Gone by eleven normally. Except Thursdays, when it's soccer—they stay all day then."

Henry, sixty-one years old, friend to the timid and scourge of the bully, appeared blinking at the cellar doorway.

"But you, now, that's different."

"I know," said Chris, a little shamefaced. "I've never done this before. I was hoping you wouldn't see me."

"I see everything," said Henry, smiling. "But whether I tell anyone what I've seen, well, that's another matter. What's so special about today that's got you sneaking out?"

"I just can't think today," said Chris.

The old man chuckled again.

"There's plenty in here can't think any day—and it's not just kids I'm talking about."

Henry's view of the school was well known. Most children were troublemakers, layabouts, and vandals, and teachers were communist infiltrators systematically destroying the morals of the youth and the fiber of the country. And both parties tramped mud through the school, into the bargain.

"I can't think because I'm going to live in Africa," Chris said, simply. "I only found out this morning."

Immediately he began, at last, to take hold of the thought. He'd been too excited to tell anyone else—

he hadn't spoken about it to anybody in his class. How do you tell your friends in a run-down London high school, with green paint peeling off the walls and drizzle blowing in through cracks in the window frames, that at eight o'clock this morning you began a journey that would end under burning sun in the most exciting and mysterious place on earth?

"Africa," he said again. "Tanzania."

And he nodded to himself as the strangeness of the thought lessened. Now that he'd told someone, it was real.

"And I can't think of anything else. How can you concentrate on quadratic equations when Africa is waiting just outside the school?"

"I can't see Africa just outside," said Henry. "I can see trash cans in the yard. And drizzle."

But he smiled gently as he said it, sharing the boy's excitement.

"I can see it. I can see the sun. I can see the blueness of the sky. And all through history, behind Snowball White's drone, there were lions roaring."

Henry laughed. "That must have kept the class quiet. They have armed police in the schools in New York, I read. Lions would be better, though the blood might upset my cleaners."

Chris joined in his laughter, enjoying the moment, enjoying sharing his great news with this kind old man.

"Africa," he said again, nodding. A statement of fact for himself. A reassurance. An affirmation.

"So," said Henry, "where are you going now? Catch the train at Clapham Common and get off at Timbuktu?"

"Not quite so far." Chris laughed. "I'm going to Charing Cross Road. To the bookshops. I don't know anything about Tanzania. I've got to find out what we're going to. I've got to get a map. Look things up. Do something. I've got to do something or I'll go mad, run amok, strangle Snowball White, and make the front page of the *Sun*."

"Good," said Henry, "I'll be able to sell my story, too."

He adopted a flat voice, like someone speaking remembered lines to a TV camera: "I knew him well—yes. A strange boy. Hardly ever played truant like the rest of the kids. Heard lions inside his head and dreamed of going to Bangladesh."

"Tanzania," said Chris. "Lions don't live in Bangladesh." He paused. Then added, "I don't think."

"Right," said Henry. "Be on your way, then. What are you wasting time here for? By the time you get to Charing Cross Road all the maps of Tanzania will be gone. There's a run on them this week. The Chelsea team has an away game there on Saturday and all the fans are going over."

"Yes," said Chris, quietly, "I heard."

Suddenly he felt a bit sad. In all the great excitement he had failed to think of one very important thing. He was going to leave on a great adventure. But leaving meant partings—and this kind old man

5

with his affectionate twinkling eyes had, in a brief flash, brought that home to him. There would be good-byes to say, loved and familiar things to leave behind, grandmas and aunts with handkerchiefs at eyes.

But that was for later, when the planning and packing were over. He'd face it when it came.

"So," said Henry, "off you go. If anyone asks, I haven't seen you."

"Thanks," Chris replied, with a grin. "We're not going until after Christmas, so I'll come and say good-bye when I leave."

"Make sure you do. And don't get run over in the meantime, it would be a waste of a plane ticket."

He turned and went through the door into the boiler room.

"You can have it if I do," called Chris, as the door was closing.

"Me? Africa? Not on your life." And Henry closed the door.

Chris shook his head and smiled.

Then he turned, crossed the yard, opened the small wooden door, and stepped into the side street.

It was a narrow, dark, dismal, dirty street.

But to Chris, on that morning, it seemed filled with burning sunlight.

Chapter 2

CHRIS HEARD THE FRONT-DOOR LATCH CLICK OPEN, AND he rushed into the hallway to greet his father.

"I thought you'd been acting a bit strangely," he said, beaming, as his father came through the door. "Now I know why. Dark horse."

Mr. Harris laughed. He dropped his bag by the hat stand, put his arm round his son's shoulders, and walked him into the living room.

"So, you've read it, have you?"

"At least four times," replied Chris. "Why didn't you say something before now?"

"Well, I didn't think I'd need to ask you whether you wanted to go, and there was no point in saying anything until it was settled. Now the contract's here, it's definite. Do I take it you approve?"

"Approve? Are you kidding? I've already bought a

map. It's on the table. Here, come and look. Show me where we're going."

"Musoma," said Mr. Harris. "That's the name of the place."

They sat at the table and studied the map. Mr. Harris traced a finger down from Nairobi and into Tanzania.

"There," he said, tapping his finger at the edge of Lake Victoria. "There it is. There's a big mission hospital there, and your dad's the new chief engineer."

"Incredible," said Chris. "Incredible. Us going to Africa. Whatever made you do it?"

"New start," replied his father. "We've both had a hard couple of years since Mom died. I'm in a rut, you don't like school—I thought we'd uproot, take the world by the throat and see what we can make of it. Agreed?"

"I'll say. I can't think of anything I'd rather do."

"That's it, then. Start thinking what you'll need. We have to send most of our things on ahead by ship, but we don't go till the first of February. That's four months, so don't get your suitcases out yet."

Four months!

One hundred and twenty days!

On that first day it could have been a century.

But time, Chris found, is a flexible thing. A day can be a year, a week can be a minute.

The map helped. It sped the days. Every day he would unfold it carefully and look at it, scanning its greens and browns and blues, savoring its names.

8

And such names! Names that sang of strangeness and smelled of Africa. Serengeti, Loliondo, Kilimanjaro, Masai Steppe. Names filled with sun and space, and warm winds carrying the tang of loping giraffe.

Sometimes it didn't seem real, didn't seem possible that this could be happening. In a comfortable English living room, fire burning, rain pattering on the windows, Africa seemed only a dream. Was it really true? Would he really see it?

But reality crept up gradually.

The days brought packing cases. Familiar and comforting things, carefully wrapped, began to fill them. Uncles visited with jokes about getting eaten by crocodiles. Sad-eyed grandmas, full of reproach and dread, fussed through the house, bringing tea cosies and calamine. Well-wishing old friends called and sat, awkward, not knowing quite what to make of the event.

And the days began to accelerate.

Christmas passed, leaving Chris a camera and binoculars. The packing cases went to the docks. Suitcases were dragged down from the attic, letters written, painful injections against terrible-sounding diseases received.

And suddenly they were ready. The bustle, the planning, the endless decisions, frustrations, excitements, brought them to the end of January. The planes circling over London took on a new significance, and in the last days of school Chris watched them endlessly from the classroom windows. Soon. Soon.

He left school on his final day by the back staircase and went to find Henry.

He knocked on the boiler-room door and went in.

Henry was seated in the ancient armchair that Eddington and "them idiots with the earrings" had stolen for him as payment for turning a blind eye to their constant truancy.

Behind the haze of smoke from his battered pipe his face lit up.

"Hello, young 'un."

"Hello, Henry."

"Come in. Come in. Sit yourself down."

Chris pulled up a stool and sat facing the old man. The room was very warm and comfortable. It smelled of coal and tobacco and pots of strong tea. The boilers hummed gently as they pumped hot water around the school.

"So, you're on your way now, I suppose?"

"Yes, Henry. We go tomorrow. Evening flight to Amsterdam. Then Africa—Kilimanjaro Airport."

Henry nodded gently.

"You're like the swallows flying south," he said. "Birds on the wing."

He paused and looked directly at the boy for a moment, then shook his head and looked away. "I always feel sad in autumn when the birds are gathering. Don't know why," he added.

He stared at the wall and it seemed to Chris that his pale eyes were seeing something beyond it.

"Yes, I know what you mean," said Chris.

"Endings and beginnings, I suppose."

"Yes."

They were silent for a moment, lost in their thoughts of journeys and Africa. An old man and a boy in a dismal London cellar caught briefly in a spell of sun and space and soft ancient winds blowing across vast plains.

And something more.

A parting. A parting not just of two people who had grown to like each other. More than that. Much more. A parting of generations, which they both recognized. The eternal parting of the young from the old. The old regretting the times gone and the opportunities missed; the young fearful but eager for the future. The old heart sinking to see the hopes of his youth made flesh in another; the young heart burning to fly away. When the old look at the young they see time made flesh and bone.

Henry looked again at Chris.

"So," he said, "fly away." They stood.

"All right," said Chris, quietly. "I'll go now. I don't know when we'll be back. I think my dad's contract is for three years."

Henry led the way and opened the door. Chris stepped out into the gray drizzle of January London.

"I'll still be here, likely," said Henry, shaking

Chris's hand. "Good luck," he added, turning back into the room, "and don't drown in the Mississippi."

"Henry, the Mississippi isn't in . . ."

But Henry had already closed the door.

Chris sighed, saddened by the good-bye. Then he began to make his way across the school yard.

High above he could hear a plane drumming down its flight path to Heathrow. He turned his head upward, but it was lost in an endless blanket of gray.

"Soon," he whispered.

And he placed his hand on the latch of the door leading into the street.

As he did so, the boiler-room door opened again.

"Hoi!" called Henry.

"Yes?"

"If you see Eddington and them idiots with the earrings, tell them the springs are poking through my chair. They'll know what to do."

Chris smiled.

Then he opened the door and stepped out on the road to Africa.

Chapter 3

KILIMANJARO AIRPORT LIES ON THE HOT SANYA PLAIN, twenty-five miles east of Arusha, twenty-five west of Moshi.

Few big planes use its massive runways now, or indeed ever have done. Built to cope with many thousands of tourists who never came, it is one of the quietest airports in the world. Tourists need luxury, and Tanzania has precious little of that. This is not tourist country, it is Masai country. There are no Rolls-Royces waiting at this airport to whisk jaded travelers to gold-plated baths in gold-plated Hiltons. Step out of your plane onto the tarmac here and you are already in the middle of the real Africa. Just beyond the airport fence the aloof, ochered Masai herd their cattle in vast, lowing dust clouds just as they have for a thousand years, oblivious to the twentieth century. Or scornful of it.

So here you enter Africa through the perfect gateway. And if you pause a moment on the tarmac and look around, your heart misses a beat.

To your left, floating it seems in the misty blue distance, is a perfect volcanic cone—Mount Meru. Rising to over four thousand five hundred meters, symmetrical and quiet against the vast African sky, it is one of the world's most beautiful mountains. Its lower slopes are covered in dense rain forest of immense age—a cool fairyland of ancient trees decked out in swathe upon swathe of hanging green mosses. Here, in this lovely, manless place, baboons and colobus monkeys pass the day's news back and forth in harsh, chattering screams; azure and gold lizards dart up and down the damp trees, quick, brilliant jewels in the forest gloom; chameleons hunt with their strange rhythmical dance, rocking from leg to leg until moths and insects are mesmerized, then, in an eye-blink, flicking out a whiplike tongue of astonishing length to haul in another luckless meal. Here, too, great crashings and splinterings warn of the presence of the world's most destructive beasts— elephants—as they smash their way through the forest, ripping whole trees apart in their constant battle to keep their great bulks nourished. And looking down over all, from unimaginable heights, circle the great birds of Africa—the eagles and buzzards, the harriers and bright bateleurs.

This, then, is a magical place. Yet it is a neglected and ignored place. A place unknown to most of the world. And the reason it is so lies to the east. Overshadowing Mount Meru and all of Africa is a mountain everyone knows. A colossus so high, so vast, so unlikely that wise men in Europe laughed in disbelief at its discovery. Kilimanjaro, the wise men said, could not exist. Snow in the tropics was impossible. Those foolish missionaries in Africa were seeing cloud, mistaking it for snow, and should get new glasses.

"There must have been some very red faces about," said Chris. He stood on the tarmac, transfixed by what he saw.

"What?" asked his father surprisedly, beside him.

"Sorry. I was thinking aloud. I was remembering the story of Kilimanjaro. How nobody believed it."

"Ah," said Mr. Harris, "yes. Red faces. You can sympathize though. I can't believe it, and I'm looking at it."

Father and son stood quietly, trying to take in what was before them.

The mountain seemed to take up the whole northeast horizon. At the nearer end the foothills rose out of the plain, gently at first, then in great thrusting folds higher and higher until suddenly, out of the folds, erupted the huge sculpted dome of ice and snow. Rearing massive and blinding in the morning sun, brilliant against the pale blue sky, the eternal snows of Kilimanjaro glinted and winked fire. A long,

15

long saddle, high and barren, drew their eyes eastward until they rested on a harsh outbreak of vicious, toothlike peaks of brown rock, snow-speckled. A frightening place of towering pinnacles, sharp points and precipices, vertiginous, awe-inspiring, dangerous.

"This end's called Kibo," said Chris. "I looked it all up on the map. It's nearly six thousand meters high at this end. The jagged end is Mawenzi. It's very dangerous there. Not climbable really. In fact, a plane crashed there years ago, I read, and there are still skeletons up there that they can't get down."

As the words sank in, father and son looked at each other, then turned and looked at the plane that had just brought them. They smiled uneasily at one another, then shuddered.

"There, but for the grace of God," said Mr. Harris. "Come on. Let's get into the terminal building; we're getting left behind."

They smiled at each other happily. The weeks of planning and waiting, the decisions, the frustrations, the fears, and anticipations were at last over.

"So, this is Africa," said Chris. "The adventure begins."

"Excited?" asked Mr. Harris.

"Are you kidding?" said Chris, and arm in arm they headed for the terminal building.

"I wonder if there's anything dangerous around here?" Chris added nervously, looking over his shoulder as they walked.

"At an airport?" said his father, incredulous. "Are you crazy?"

He was wrong. Just outside the airport, jostling and snarling, a feared and lethal threat awaited.

Tanzanian taxis.

Chris and his father, unsuspectingly making their way through the airport formalities, were about to discover just how dangerous life in Africa can be.

As they emerged from the main door they were instantly surrounded and deafened.

"Bwana. Taxi, bwana. This one, bwana. Arusha, bwana. Moshi, bwana. Very reliable. This one, bwana. Very cheap. Take mine, bwana."

The cheerful, ragged taxi drivers grabbed their bags out of their hands, tugged their shirts, pushed, guided, jostled, and cajoled the bewildered father and son toward the taxis.

"Taxis?" gasped Chris. "Are they taxis?"

Before them was an amazing assortment of junk-yard vehicles with windshields missing, odd wheels, wrong hoods, bald tires. The noise was astounding, the condition of the vehicles appalling, the sun blinding. In the confusion Mr. Harris could not remember the name of the hotel.

"Er, yes. Arusha, er, New Something Hotel."

He felt in his pocket for the piece of paper with the hotel name and address, but the good-natured riot was ahead of him.

"New Safari. New Safari. New Safari."

The cry went up to screaming pitch as all the Arusha drivers pushed forward.

"Me, bwana. This way, bwana. New Safari, bwana."

Amidst all the din a fight broke out, to the delight of all the other drivers, who started whooping and jeering, and the two bewildered, astonished travelers were pushed relentlessly by a huge, grinning man into the back of an ancient purple car whose front passenger seat was entirely missing.

"OK, bwana, don't worry. You wait there." The driver beamed joyfully. "New Safari straightaway."

He winked hugely at Chris, turned, gave an ear-piercing whoop, and hurled himself back into the mêlée of riotous, grinning drivers, emerging breathless seconds later carrying all the Harris luggage.

"OK, bwana, don't worry," he yelled. "You're lucky. These people, they are snakes. They will cheat you. I, Josephu, do not cheat. New Safari. Straightaway."

And he crashed the trunk lid down onto the luggage with a force that shook the car from end to end.

Chris glanced nervously at his father.

Josephu thumped his large body down into the driver's seat, slammed the door with another head-shattering crash, and jammed it with a piece of wood to stop it falling open.

"I've never seen a car like this," whispered Chris.

"I don't think anyone has," replied his father. "It looks as if it's made up out of bits."

"OK, you snakes," Josephu bellowed. "PUSH!"

Still making a huge cacophonous din, the grinning, arguing, jostling crowd surrounded the car.

"But," said Chris hesitantly, "your engine's running. Why do you need a push?"

"Ha," yelled the driver happily. "No first gear. No second gear. Only third and fourth. Anyway—no clutch. So, these snakes, they will push. We go fast and bang, into third gear and we go."

"Ah," said Chris.

"Oh," said Mr. Harris.

"Don't worry. I, Josephu, will get you there OK. This car—good car. *Push*, snakes."

And push they did, down the road, gathering speed around a parking lot until, running at top speed— CRASH—the gear went in, the engine roared, the car lurched crazily and accelerated down the airport exit road. The cheers of the mob receded behind them, and their noise was replaced by an astonishing mixture of groans, creaks, bangs, clanks, wheezes, grindings, and thumps as Josephu set the ancient car thundering down the dead center of the road at seventy miles an hour.

Suddenly, Mr. Harris sat bolt upright.

"My God," he said. "There's a crossroad coming up." His voice rose. "There's a truck."

To the right Chris saw that there was indeed a huge semi truck bearing rapidly down to where the airport road joined the main road. He glanced at the driver, who was now happily engaged in singing and gazing around.

"Slow down. There's a truck," screamed Chris. His hands were bunched into white-knuckled fists.

Josephu glanced to the right, revved the engine ferociously, and ground and crashed the gears from fourth back into third.

"Can't slow," he shouted. "Not enough gears. Don't worry. We beat him."

And, whooping with joy, he hurtled the car toward the crossroad, still at seventy miles an hour.

The truck bore implacably down toward the fatal meeting point.

Help, thought Chris. *We're not going to survive even ten minutes in Africa.*

"Don't worreeee," yelled Josephu, like a kamikaze pilot, as the car and truck converged.

As he reached the crossroad he gave a brief stamp on the brake, then flung the car into a ninety-degree left turn onto the main road. The tires screamed in fury, and the car threatened to turn onto its side as both passenger-side wheels came off the ground.

Terrified, Chris glanced to the right. What he saw at that moment would live with him forever. Filling the whole of his window was the massive truck radiator, so close he could clearly see dead moths and insects splattered against the grille. So close he could smell, he thought, the heat of the engine. So close he involuntarily yelped in horror and fear.

And then, miraculously, it was over. Josephu hit the accelerator hard, flinging the car straight around into the center of the road, where it righted itself, shaking from side to side like a wet dog. With an angry screech of brakes and great blarings of a horn, the truck fell in behind the car, only millimeters separating their bumpers.

Completely unperturbed, Josephu began to accelerate away. He wound the car up to seventy again and rammed it into fourth with a thunderous crash that threatened to tear the gearbox out of the car. He was happily singing the current hit "Do You Remember Zion?"

"I'll give him Zion," snarled Chris's father under his breath.

The driver turned, grinned massively, and said, "OK. Don't worry. New Safari—straightaway."

Chapter 4

OUTSIDE THE NEW SAFARI HOTEL IN ARUSHA, MIKE TAY-lor was busy loading the Land Rover. It was a lucky week. An American tourist had booked him for a safari out to Serengeti, so for the first time in many weeks there would be some money coming in.

Life had become harder and harder recently. Somewhere, he reflected, Tanzania had gone wrong. The greatest game parks in the world were being bypassed by the tourists in favor of Kenya. Kenya was swamped with tourists while Tanzania was deserted. The safari crowd have a saying that if you see a lion in Kenya he will be surrounded by twenty tourists; if you see a tourist in Tanzania he will be surrounded by twenty lions.

There was a lot of truth in it. Tanzania, one of the poorest countries in the world, was falling further and further behind. There were few precious dollars for imports, so the shops were empty; buses and tractors broke down and stayed that way; the towns and the roads were collapsing; electricity failed regularly; water came through the taps only spasmodically; and gasoline had been rationed for months.

It was gasoline that was taking up Mike Taylor's attention at this moment. He was surrounded by jerricans, twenty of them in all—the fruits of wheeling and dealing on the black market and some well-placed bribes. By sheer guile, cunning, and dishonesty he now had enough gasoline to take his safari to Seronera and back. He felt well satisfied with his morning's work.

He was passing the heavy cans up, one by one, to Bennie, his Chagga driver, who was standing on the roof rack.

"Where are we going, boss?"

"We're taking an American out to Seronera. He's very rich, so I'd be obliged if you'd try to be polite for a change. We might get a fat tip then."

Bennie's face split into a huge grin.

"Me, polite, boss? I'm always polite. Especially to Americans. Americans have dollars." His eyes shone at the word.

"You're a rogue. You've always been a rogue. And if you upset this man like you did the last, I'm going to sack you."

"Aw, boss, come on. It was a joke."

"Putting a snake in a tourist's camera bag is not a

joke. He might have had a heart attack. Then where would we have been? In jail, the pair of us."

Bennie grinned even more broadly.

"Boss, it was a harmless tree snake. And you laughed so hard you fell over. I saw you."

Mike glared through narrowed eyes.

"Shut up—and load the gas."

"Yes, boss."

They continued in silence for several minutes until the last of the cans was in place.

"OK, you chain those down now, or they'll all be gone before we can look around. I'll go and get the guns and see if our passenger's ready."

Mike turned and crossed the road to the hotel entrance. He was just passing through the main door when Bennie called.

"Anyway, we wouldn't have been put in jail."

"Why not?"

"The police chief is my uncle."

Mike snarled once, then stepped into the dimness of the New Safari Hotel.

"New" was not the best description. In fact, the New Safari Hotel could be said to have had its day. Once splendid, it had started to fall into disrepair years ago—and no one had bothered to stop it falling.

Now the walls peeled and cracked. The carpets and huge leather chairs were full of holes. Overhead, sulky fans stirred up clouds of mosquitoes that whined and whirred constantly. Cockroaches scurried everywhere, their obscene antennae waving, their prehistoric shells crunching sickeningly underfoot.

Everything smelled. Of age, damp, the tropics, dirt, and decay.

Mike crossed to the huge bar, a solid, carved-wood construction backed by cracked and brown-spotted mirrors. The bar shelves were empty. In good times you could get Konyagi, a powerful local liquor. Once in a blue moon, you could get Coca-Cola.

These weren't good times, and there was only Safari Lager, the local beer.

"Beer."

The barman handed Mike a warm brown bottle, and Mike held it up to the light to see if any cockroaches had found their way in. Long years in the tropics had given him a loathing of these creatures. And also a grudging respect. Once he'd opened a jar of cayenne pepper that he knew had not been opened for a year—out had crawled a bright orange cockroach.

"Things that can survive like that will be here when everything else has gone," Mike was prone to say.

Satisfied that the beer contained nothing unusual, he selected the leather armchair that seemed to have the fewest springs poking out and slumped his long bony frame into it.

To anyone knowing him by his reputation alone, he would have come as something of a disappointment.

He had been, for many years, chief game warden in Tanzania's great, lonely Selous game reserve. This vast, remote, wild, and haunting place had been one of the last great wildernesses on earth, and Mike had given his heart to the place and to the shy and peaceful animals living there.

It was well known that he preferred the animals to his fellow men. Well known that he would shoot an animal only in defense or if it was wounded, but would, without hesitation or emotion, shoot poachers dead. He was a man reputed to be afraid of nothing; a man who devoted his life to protecting the wild beauty of Tanzania; a man who knew more about that vast country than any man alive.

Such a man, you would be forgiven for thinking, would be impressive. He would look like Robert Redford, immaculate in safari khaki, leopard-skin band around a wide-brimmed bush hat, elephant-hair bracelet on his wrist, pale blue eyes gazing forever at distant horizons. A bronze god.

The man slumped in the chair, grimacing at his warm beer, didn't look anything like that at all.

True, the years in the tropics had burned his arms and legs to a deep walnut. But they had also drained the color from his face. Years of malaria and dysentery had left him skeletally thin, his skin faintly yellow-sheened. The sun had drawn the life out of his hair and beard, and both were now prematurely pure white. He wore a T-shirt that had been left behind by a tourist two years ago and which bore the letters UCLA (he could not have told you what they stood for), baggy khaki shorts, and white tennis shoes with no socks.

The pale blue eyes were another matter: Those he did have, and they were constantly looking at far distant horizons. Horizons of the past.

His job at Selous had come to an end five years ago. Government indifference, lack of money to keep up the road and the Land Rovers, increasingly daring and sophisticated poachers, frequently helped by the local people, all had combined to drive him away from his beloved reserve and his animals. He could not bear to be there watching over the slow destruction of his years of work and care, so he simply turned his back and left.

He'd tried going "home" to England. He had almost gone mad with claustrophobia there, dreaming constantly of the great spaces and endless skies of his Africa. So he had come back, with a Land Rover, and settled into a comfortable rut driving tourists out to take photos of obliging and patient lions.

He sighed heavily as he remembered.

"A fond farewell to all my greatness," he muttered into his beer bottle. "Still, it's not too bad, I suppose." And he chuckled at the thought of the snake. "Thank heavens for Bennie, anyway."

Almost on cue Bennie appeared in the doorway.

"All finished, *mzee*. Gas is tied down. Water tanks are full. Bags are all in. We go, eh?"

"We go," said Mike.

He walked across to the bar. Reaching over he pulled out two long, leather-cased rifles from under the bar and winked at the barman.

"Thanks for looking after them."

The barman acknowledged him with a grin.

"Did you know," asked Mike, "that Ernest Hemingway used to keep his guns behind that very bar?"

"Who?" said Bennie.

"Don't pretend to be ignorant. Someday someone will believe you are. You know very well who I'm talking about."

"Sorry," said Bennie.

The barman grinned again. "Him," he said. "Once he got drunk in here and fired a shotgun at the ceiling. The shots went straight up through the floor of a bedroom, through the mattress, and into a fat white lady's backside. She came running down the stairs in her nightgown and knocked Hemingway to the floor."

He whooped joyfully at the picture he'd created, and Bennie joined in. Fat women were always fair game for laughter.

"Just think," said Mike when they'd calmed down, "I may be standing on the very spot where Hemingway stood. Or fell down."

The three regarded the floorboards, but they revealed nothing of the great man of literature and riot. So Mike said with finality, "OK. We go. Bennie, go up and tell our customer we're ready. He's in

room fourteen and his name's Hyram T. Johnson.
Be polite. Call him 'Sir.' "

"OK, boss."

"And Bennie."

"Yes, boss?"

"Keep out of his bags."

"OK, boss."

And Bennie left, a wide and completely innocent
grin on his face.

Guns under his arm, Mike strolled through the
squalid hotel lobby. Reaching the main doorway, he
placed his hand on the swing door that opened out
onto the street. As he did so the door suddenly
crashed open with a violence that threw him backward. Tripping on the cracked and buckled tile floor-
ing, he flung out his arms toward the wall to stop
himself falling. The guns crashed to the ground.

Briefly blinded by the brilliant light flooding in
from the street, he recovered to see a large, black
form striding across the lobby, massively laden with
suitcases and bags.

He cursed under his breath.

A voice said, "Oh dear. Are you all right?"

Mike shook his head sharply to clear his vision
and found himself looking at an earnest, fair-haired
boy of about fourteen.

"What the devil was that?" he asked. "An
earthquake?"

"Sort of." The boy laughed. "You should see him

drive. Here, let me get these for you." He gathered up the two leather cases and handed them to Mike.

"Careful," said Mike, "they're guns. Put them on this table. We'll have a look and see if the fool's damaged them."

"Guns?" said the boy, greatly impressed. He stared at the angular, eccentric-looking figure before him. "Are you . . . a hunter?"

"No, not really," said Mike, "though I might make an exception for him." He glowered darkly across the lobby to where Josephu was enthusiastically crashing bags about and bellowing amiably at the receptionist.

Mr. Harris came through the door.

"What's going on?" he asked. He sounded very irritable.

"It's that driver," said Chris. "He didn't kill anyone on the road, but he's still trying."

"Oh," said Mr. Harris, and he slumped into a chair.

Mike had finished checking the guns.

"Well, no harm done. They look OK."

He looked more closely now at the father and son.

"You tourists?" he asked.

"No," replied Chris, "we're coming to live here. We've just arrived on the morning plane from Amsterdam. My father's going to be the engineer at Musoma Hospital. We're flying out there this afternoon on a missionary plane."

Mike extended his hand.

"Welcome to Tanzania, then. My name's Mike Taylor. You're going the same way as me. I'm driving out to Seronera with a tourist today. You'll pass over there. It's a huge hotel built into the rocks of a kopje. The pilot will point it out to you. You can give me a wave."

"I'll do that," said Chris.

"If you're ever in Arusha again, look out for me. Look for a white Land Rover with Taylor's Tours on the side. I'll buy you a Coke, if this country ever gets any again."

And with a brief nod and a smile he turned to leave. He paused a second at the door and turned again.

"What's your name, by the way?"

"Chris Harris."

And Mike stepped out of the doorway onto the street.

Chris whistled. "What a strange character," he said.

"I've had enough characters for one day," grumbled Mr. Harris. "Enough taxis for a year, and after this next one I won't want to see another airplane for a long time. Let's see if we can get two or three hours' sleep before the next stretch."

Sleep? thought Chris. *How could anyone want to sleep at a time like this?*

He walked to the window and looked out. Brightly dressed people filled the street, a moving tapestry of color lit up by the brilliant morning sun. It was hard to believe that only yesterday they had left the fog and bitter cold of winter London.

He stood for some time watching Mike Taylor helping the overdressed and sweating tourist into his Land Rover.

Interesting man, he thought to himself. *I hope I run into him again.*

Chapter 5

THE PRIDE HAD HUNTED THAT MORNING. PREY WAS plentiful now. The wildebeest were migrating, and long skeins of them filled the skylines, a million gargoyle shapes on a strange pilgrimage to nowhere. In the predawn darkness the pride had isolated a cow, circling her, padding softly closer and closer until she stood transfixed with terror and bewilderment, eyes wildly searching the night. In a swift, snarling flurry they had brought her down, tearing pieces of her flesh before the last terrible bolt of fear had died in her brain.

The luminous light of the Serengeti morning now lit the scene. The old male, battle-scarred and thinning with age, had wandered off to the kopje close by and spread himself on his favorite rock. Below him his lionesses and the two cubs were still feeding, grunting and snarling their pleasure at the bloody carcass.

A little way off, waiting his turn, the young male pretender crouched in a stalking pose, tail threshing from side to side in impatience.

The old male's lips curled back as his eyes lighted on the younger lion, and he gave a low, warning snarl. The pretender returned it with one of challenge but did not move.

Farther off still, slavering and chittering, constantly moving back and forth, the hyenas circled. Round and round, in and out, slinking and snickering, they performed an obscene ballet, their ferocious, bone-crunching jaws working in anticipation of the delights to come.

And overhead the ageless, sky-borne symbol of death in Africa, the vultures, insane-eyed and vile, beat lazy, patient circles in the sky.

The eternal daily scene of Africa. One of a million deaths a day, unwitnessed by man, unmourned by anything.

The young male half rose, impatient. Head down, he started a slow, stalking advance toward the feeding group. Two steps; another two; another.

The old patriarch, from high on the kopje, saw him at once. He lifted his head backward to the sky, opened his great mouth, and gave a single, air-shattering bark of warning.

The pretender stopped. It hadn't been a serious

move anyway. It was part of the daily ritual. A ritual of challenge and rebuttal, feints and passes, advances and retreats. The meaning was clear to all. The old, his powers failing, would soon be replaced by the new. Driven out by the young, strong blood that would sire the next generation. Already the lionesses were showing signs that they did not mind the attentions of this new, powerful force.

But the time was not quite yet. The old lion could still summon an awesome majesty, still deliver a cuff that would knock this impertinent youngster into the dust and send him whining sulkily out beyond the invisible truce line to nurse his bruises.

It didn't matter—the pretender had plenty of time to wait.

The lionesses finished eating. With stomachs so distended they hung almost to the ground, they slowly began to usher the cubs to the kopje. Leaping heavily upward from rock to rock, they arranged themselves below their patriarch, who sleepily grunted a welcome.

Now it was the pretender's turn.

With a sudden violence the young lion rose, turned, and hurled himself at the uneasily swirling hyena pack, barking a warning as he went. In a harsh, gibbering screech of terror the pack scattered, dust flying, and settled in a tightly moving, complaining knot some distance off.

The warning delivered, the lion turned his back

on the noisy complainants and, with a lazy, stately tread, paced slowly back toward his bloody breakfast table.

A quiet settled on the still Serengeti morning. A lull until the well-rehearsed scene change.

The silence was broken only by the grunts of the feeding lion and the soft hiss of patient vulture wings.

Chapter 6

THE TINY, SINGLE-ENGINED PLANE WHIRRED LIKE A
sewing machine, gathering speed down the runway
and lifting easily and smoothly into the air. Climbing
steadily, the pilot banked the plane to the right, circling over Arusha town.

From his seat beside the pilot, Chris looked down.
Everywhere was color. The whitewashed houses
with their red pantile roofs sat in avenues of brilliant
violet-flowered jacaranda trees and gardens hedged
with purple and scarlet bougainvillea. Ancient cars
and huge, brightly painted buses snaked their way
through the crowds of vividly dressed people. Bright-
ness—that had been Chris's first impression of an
African town. Vivid colors of flowers and plants were
taken up and mimicked in African dress, so that the
whole town was an artist's palette of colors. "A riot

of color," Chris had read somewhere. "Riot" was the correct word. Color here was almost violent.

The plane came around in a full circle and leveled as the pilot set a course due west toward the center of Africa and to the place that was to be their home for the next three years.

Within minutes the town and its dark green borders of coffee plantations had fallen away behind them. It was now four o'clock in the afternoon and the sun, still well up in the sky, had become more friendly. A golden yellow had replaced the terrible whiteness of its noonday heat.

As Chris looked ahead from the cockpit, then left to the south, then north, suddenly, like a hammer blow, Africa hit him with a numbing force.

It wasn't just the immensely long vistas stretching in each direction, though these were stunning enough. He felt, in the luminous light air, that he could see for a thousand miles, and distant mountains floated in pastel blues and pinks at the edges of the world. But it was not just the size that was the force hitting him as he took his first real look at this land. It was the vast, heart-stopping emptiness. To eyes used to cities and towns or the well-ordered, neat fields and hedgerows and snaking roads of England, the great lonelinesses and silences of Africa drove a shaft of fear through him.

For a second Chris shuddered. Suddenly, in this tiny plane, he realized how insulated from danger all his past life had been. This, now in front of him, was a land unchanged for tens of thousands of years.

He could not have put his fear into words, but deep down inside him his race memory was telling him that here was danger. That here, behind a tree or rock, from a hole in the ground or sliding just below the surface of the water, from the long grass or from the air, there was threat. Death is in the air you breathe in Africa, and those who do not heed its smell do not survive.

The shudder passed, but Chris turned his eyes away from the windows and looked instead at the pilot for reassurance. Africa had given him a fright. Had, in a flash of realization, shaken his security. Suddenly he felt very young and helpless.

The pilot grinned at him. "What's up, lad, got the heebie-jeebies?"

Chris nodded. "Yes," he said sheepishly, as he realized that the pilot had seen him shiver. "It was too sudden. One minute we were over the town. The next minute—nothing."

He turned in his seat and looked at his father to see if he had had the same reaction. Mr. Harris was looking out of the window, serious-faced but calm.

"Don't worry," said the pilot, "it affects lots of people that way the first time."

"It's so empty," said Chris.

"Not a bit of it. It only looks that way. It's full. Keep your eyes open for the next hour and you'll see more animals than you've seen in your life. Hang on to your seat, and I'll take you to see some friends of mine."

And with a wide grin he flung the plane into a banking, left-hand dive.

"Look ahead. See the lake?"

Chris nodded. Shimmering in the distance a silver patch, edged with pink, lay on the plain. Behind it rose a solid green wall stretching north to south as far as the eye could see.

"Lake Manyara and the Rift Valley wall." The pilot had to shout over the noise of the engine.

The plane leveled out at about one hundred and fifty feet. Close to, the land looked less forbidding, and Chris, confidence restored by the pilot's amiable good nature and obvious capability, settled back.

He hadn't been too impressed with flying so far. After his initial amazement at the vast size of the DC-10, he'd been disappointed to find that there was precious little excitement on a long-haul flight. Nothing to see at all. Nothing to do except eat and sleep.

But this. This was different. Barreling along almost at treetop height, banking and swerving, the smell of hot oil and aviation fuel in his nostrils—this was really flying. The roaring of the engine, and the ground and trees hurtling below, gave him the exhilaration of a roller-coaster ride. He grinned.

"That's better. Now watch."

The end of the lake came flying up at them, and Chris was astonished to see the pink edges resolve themselves into a multitude of single dots. As the plane shot over them, a million heads with preposterously large black beaks turned upward. Flamingos. Countless numbers of pink-and-white forms, dipping and sifting the edges of the lake, elegantly high-stepping on matchstick, ballet-dancer legs.

Almost skimming the surface of the water, the plane shot straight across the center of the lake. A few flamingos, startled, took off into the air—huge, ungainly fliers, necks bent into S-shapes, legs like broken twigs trailing, helpless-looking, behind.

Then they were over the land again, with a small, sluggish river, brown and soupy, snaking off in front of them.

"This is where my friends live. Keep your eyes on the river."

The pilot throttled back; the plane slowed and they followed the bank along.

"There," he said. "Straight ahead."

Chris followed the pilot's eyes. The river opened out into a large pool filled with round gray rocks. A few birds lined the edges, and one or two sat preening themselves on the rocks.

Hmm, thought Chris, *he must be a bird-watcher. First the flamingos—now these*. He was a little disappointed; birds were all right, but . . . At that moment one of the rocks raised a huge, warty head out of the water and yawned. A great pink cavern of a mouth and stumpy teeth gazed up at them as the plane whooshed directly over the pool.

"That'll wake them up," shouted the pilot, happily. "Lazy blighters, hippos."

And he brought the plane right around and headed back toward the pool.

Chris turned in his seat and shouted above the engine noise.

"Dad, look. Hippos!"

Mr. Harris smiled at his son's excitement.

"I see them," he called back.

This time there was more activity. Startled by the low-flying plane, a few of the huge creatures had hauled themselves out of the water and were standing uneasily at the pool edges. Chris noticed a calf hiding between two cows and called, "Oh look, they've got a calf—don't frighten them."

"They're not frightened—just curious about the noise. And don't be fooled by that timid look. If we went near that calf they'd bite us in two."

Once more the plane roared over them, and even above the noise of the engine Chris could hear a great commotion of honkings and hootings and brayings of complaint from below as a hundred heads swung with surprising ease and lightness to follow them across the sky.

"OK. Last time," said the pilot as he swung the plane around again.

This time some big bull hippos had finally dragged themselves out onto the banks. As the plane headed back toward them, one detached himself from the herd and trotted toward the sound, blinking myopically, head high.

"How amazing. I thought they were clumsy creatures," exclaimed Chris. "He's trotting just like a horse. Just as graceful."

"I know," said the pilot, looking down, almost affectionately, at the big bull. "They really are quite nimble, you know. They'll run you down easily if they want to. Underwater they're even better. Superb swimmers."

And the plane shot over them for the last time, leaving them to grumble and argue their way back into the coolness of the water.

Chris turned in his seat, wishing he were able to stay, and watched them sliding their huge bulks back into the cool depths.

Now the plane was climbing again. The hippo pool detour had brought them close to the Rift Valley wall, and the plane was flying along parallel to the wall to gain height.

"Next stop, the Ninth Wonder of the World," shouted the pilot.

"Ninth? What's the eighth?"

"You're looking at it. The Rift. A valley that stretches four thousand miles. From the Dead Sea to Mozambique, straight down Africa. Cracked the country nearly from top to bottom. Imagine the bang when the floor fell out of this."

Chris looked at the sheer two-thousand-foot valley-side and marveled. He realized the land they had been flying over, the valley floor, had once been level with the top of this cliff. He tried to imagine a slice of land four thousand miles long and fifty miles wide simply falling with a bang, but the thought was too big.

The pilot chuckled at the bewilderment on Chris's face.

"Think big," he shouted. "Everything in Africa is big."

The plane shot up now over the lip of the Rift wall and began to turn, still climbing rapidly.

"So—what's the ninth?"

"The ninth is coming up now. Look ahead."

The plane swung around, and in the distance Chris saw the blue bulk of a high, rounded mountain against the skyline.

"What, the hill?" he asked.

"That 'hill,' as you call it, my young friend, is the Ninth Wonder. The world's largest zoo."

"Zoo?" echoed Chris, incredulous.

"You'll see. Sit back. We've some climbing to do. That's Ngorongoro Crater, and we've got to get up to ten thousand feet to get into it."

"Crater? You mean it's a volcano?" There was alarm in Chris's voice, and he glanced back at his father. Fortunately Mr. Harris couldn't hear much for the noise of the engine and simply smiled calmly back at him.

44

"Relax. It's been extinct for thousands of years. Just wait and watch."

And the plane climbed steadily. And climbed; up and up and up, until at ten thousand feet they leveled out and headed toward the mountain. Gradually it became apparent that it was indeed a crater, but a crater so vast it defied the imagination. A miraculous rust-red road drove its way upward through the dense rain forest to the rim and, on a dizzy knife-edge, circled away around to the west.

The plane shot over the road, over the last line of trees clinging desperately in thin air.

"There," said the pilot, triumphant.

Chris gasped, his mind spinning, dizzied by what he saw.

This was a crater?

"But . . ." He stopped, not knowing what to say. Again a chill struck him. Again the vastness was almost beyond comprehension.

The crater wall plummeted sheer downward thousands of feet to the crater floor. Yet it didn't seem like a crater—more like a huge, green, fertile valley— for the other side was so far away it was almost like another separate mountain in the distance.

"Think big," said the pilot, quietly this time. "This is the biggest."

"How big?" asked Chris.

"From wall to wall, straight across, it's ten miles. And twelve miles long."

The plane was falling now, down, down toward the crater floor, almost gliding, with the throttle eased right off. The cockpit had become quiet. Even from a plane it was obvious that this was a magical place. A place shut off from the world.

A lost valley.

"What did you mean, 'the greatest zoo in the world'?" Chris asked.

"Look around. We're completely surrounded now by the crater walls. Not impossible to get in or out, but difficult. The grass is good, the trees strong. There's water—even a lake down there, see. If you were an animal, wouldn't you want to live here?"

And now, as the plane neared the ground, Chris could see what he meant. Here, in this vast bowl, was all of African life at peace with itself. As they skimmed along they could see great herds of zebra and gazelle grazing quietly on the heavy, bright grasses; wildebeest lying like farm cows chewing the cud; giraffe loping, simultaneously ponderous and smooth, dwarfing the trees; and away to the west, like great moving boulders, elephants happily tearing at the massive trunks of baobab trees. They seemed to take no notice at all of the plane.

"They're all here," said the pilot. "Lion, cheetah, leopard. All the hunters and grazers alike. Even the poor rhino find safety here."

"Safety? From what?"

"From the most vicious animal of all. From the only animal who kills for pleasure or greed."

He glanced at Chris.

"Safety from man."

Chris nodded.

"For years anything that moved in this country was likely to be shot. 'Fair game,' they called it." He scowled heavily. "Do you know, Lord Delamere once brought a hunting party from Nairobi onto Serengeti, and they shot one hundred lions in one day. Imagine. The most noble beasts on this earth dying in agony just to keep bored civil servants entertained. Like shooting ducks at a fairground rifle range."

They fell silent.

Mr. Harris tapped Chris on the shoulder.

"Look down there," he called. "To the left."

Below, a lone rhino padded softly across a clearing, turning his head slightly to the engine noise, his huge, prehistoric form so strange, so primeval.

"Look at him," said the pilot. "The saddest sight in the world. His kind have been hunted to the edge of extinction. They kill him just for his horn. The Chinese powder it and eat it. They think it brings back their youth."

"Does it?" asked Chris.

"I don't know—or care. Who's going to bring back all the rhinos, that's what I want to know?"

Savagely he yanked the throttle open again, and the plane surged into a steep climb out of the crater.

"Anyway, see what I mean about the zoo? At least the game wardens can protect the animals here, and it's too steep for the poachers to be bothered. They stay out on Serengeti where there's less chance of being caught."

The plane was climbing rapidly now.

"Sometimes I think it would be best if man was the one to become extinct. Everything else would stand a chance then."

And he rocketed the plane out over the far rim and onto Serengeti. He busied himself a moment with chart and compass, then set a course north, northwest, putting the now lowering sun on their left.

"OK. Musoma here we come," he said.

Chris glanced at his watch. It was now 4:45 P.M.

"Just over an hour from here," the pilot said. "Straight across Serengeti now. We'll pass over a big hotel called Seronera Lodge in about half an hour."

"That's where Mike Taylor said he was going. A man I met in Arusha this morning. Do you know him?"

"Oh yes." The pilot grinned. "Everyone knows him. Especially poachers."

He gave a satisfied nod.

"The animals don't know it, but they've got a one-man army protecting them there."

"He told me to look out for him. Might we see him on the road?"

"Well, we'll follow the road for a while as we get farther north—but for the next fifty miles or so, there's nothing. So, sit back, relax and enjoy the flight, as the jumbo captains say. I'll keep low so we'll see anything of interest."

48

They fell quiet, each lost in his own thoughts, as the plane drummed steadily across the seemingly infinite emptiness. The sun had reddened now, and the cockpit was bathed with a soporific glow. Chris felt his eyes growing heavy, but he glued himself to the window. He wasn't going to miss anything. He did as the pilot suggested—sat back, relaxed, and watched.

His eyes drifted out over the flat-topped acacia trees dotting the endless landscape, and he felt the immense sadness of Africa wash over him. A new dimension had been added, the inhumanity of man in this savage land. He could not shift from his mind the picture of the solitary, anxious rhino padding out his life, a hair's breadth from being the last of his kind. He was unable to conceive the mind that could kill so great and majestic a beast for such trivial gain.

Another lesson learned, he thought to himself.

And the plane continued its steady beat, a background to his thoughts.

Ahead of them, an aging lion lifted his head slightly. His still-keen ears had picked up an alien, droning sound out over the drowsy late afternoon.

He growled low, a warning to the rest of the pride, and they all stirred, grumbling with sleep, but instantly alert.

The drone came nearer—louder.

Sensing danger now, the old lion rose and looked

out over the plain. He saw nothing—but still the sound came nearer.

He dropped down the kopje from rock to rock and padded out toward the sound. The lionesses herded the cubs into a hollow behind a large boulder and sat snarling, tails twitching.

Just out from the kopje the wildebeest carcass was a boiling mass of vultures still squabbling over the last remains.

Now the sound was very loud and approaching fast.

The lion threw back his massively maned head and let out a chilling boom of challenge. Instantly the startled vultures rose into the air in a shrill, screaming cloud: a hundred grotesque shapes.

At that precise moment, roaring at one hundred feet out of the reddening light of Serengeti, without the possibility of evading action, head-on at one hundred and thirty miles an hour, into the black cloud of heavy, distended, gorged and screaming birds, came a small, fragile, silver plane.

Chapter 7

THE ROOM WAS VERY DARK, YET HE KNEW WHERE HE was instantly. The big old armchair stood, shadowed heavily, in the corner, its springs poking out, violent and murderous-looking. The huge boilers drummed heavily, and a dull, red heat emanated from them. He was back at school, in Henry's room.

But it was not the friendly, welcoming room he remembered. Menace was everywhere. Shadows flitted and swooped. The chair was bigger, much bigger, and the rips in the upholstery twisted themselves into leering mouths, slack-lipped with mockery. The fire tools leaning against the boilers juddered insanely against each other, rattling like dungeon chains as they danced to the drum of the boilers.

Outside, beyond the closed door, he could hear a rustling, a padding of huge, soft feet, a harsh, hungry breathing. Something knew he was in there and paced impatiently, waiting for him. A cloying stench of animal seeped under the door, and the boy gagged at the heavy blood smell.

He could not move. He seemed to be weighed down by a huge invisible force pushing him into the floor. A bolt of panic shot through him. What had happened? One minute he had been talking quietly with Henry in the familiar, comforting room; the next he was lying, paralyzed it seemed, in this nightmare place of evil and horror. What could possibly have occurred?

Desperately he tried to rise—his head lifting painfully an inch or two off the floor. His head hurt. Badly, very badly. He tried to bring up his right arm to explore the pain. His arm would not move.

The drumming from the boilers was becoming heavier, becoming a rhythmic thud that shook his head. The redness was intensifying. He could feel and sense the terrible heat and power building up inside them.

The stink of animal was growing, too. A low, impatient snarl rumbled chillingly just outside the door. Then a thud, which juddered the door in its frame, and a long fearful scrape as great claws gouged deep grooves in the wood.

Animal breath rasped—urgent with blood lust.

In terror Chris summoned all his force and willpower into his body.

"Roll," he commanded himself. "Roll."

Panic gave him strength and, painfully, he lurched himself over onto his right shoulder. Now he could see more clearly. The boilers were shaking crazily, the red heat turning to white. Flames were beginning to lick around their bases, casting great shadows outward to dance a mad, grotesque ballet on the walls.

He lay, gasping for strength, his mind screaming with fear at the insanity of it all.

Through the blinding fear and pain he became aware of a faint voice calling from far, far away.

"Chris. Chris, boy. Get out—now. Get out of there."

It was a voice he knew well. It was Henry's voice. But where was Henry? Why wasn't he here, helping him? He'd been here only a minute ago.

"Get out. Get to the door. GET OUT!"

Agonizingly slowly he stretched out his arms and, with a heave, rolled over onto his stomach. The pain from his head flashed through his eyes, but his fear drove him to superhuman strength. He pushed hard with his palms on the floor and forced himself up onto his knees. Then, slowly, desperately slowly, he began to inch toward the door.

"Good," called the voice from a thousand miles away. "Good boy. Now go. Go. Get out!"

The boilers now were searing, white-hot tubes of metal, their heat scorching him as he crawled. Molten metal was beginning to drip from them, the drops exploding into showers of sparks as they hit the floor. The whole room now seemed to be jumping and crashing around him, the floor bucking beneath his knees.

"Open the door," called Henry. "Open it. Quickly. They're ready to blow."

Chris reached up and placed his hand on the latch. The heat of the room was unbearable now, and his clothes were starting to smolder. Any moment now would be flash point, and the room and he would go up together.

The latch clicked under the pressure of his hand.

Instantly Chris's heart was frozen by a great screaming roar of triumph. A roar so terrible, so primordially savage, it drove down into his soul. The roar of a hunter at the point of a kill.

He was trapped. Completely, irreversibly trapped.

Trapped between the fires of hell behind him—and the devil beyond the door.

He hesitated. But only for a split second. He had no choice. This room was certain, fiery, agonizing death.

He had to risk what was beyond that door.

With both hands now on the latch he dragged himself up onto his feet and braced himself to throw the door open.

"It's all right."

The voice was shouting urgently now over the terrible crashing from the room.

"Trust me. It's all right. Go. GO!"

And he flung the door wide and fell out into the night. Scrambling now, his hands and knees torn and bleeding, his breath whimpering with fear, he pulled himself away from the room and its consuming fire.

As he crawled away his eyes wildly searched the night landscape.

Where was it? Where was the thing at the door?

Now he found himself in another nightmare.

A weird, alien place. Quiet and moon-bathed. Tortured trees twisting, hideously black, against the skyline. Heavy, dark shapes moved in and out of the trees, and red eyes glowed evilly in the darkness beyond.

A sob of horror escaped him as his eyes moved around from the trees. There, on this terrible plain, bone white in the cold moon-glow, sat a huge, human skull.

Terror began to shake Chris's body.

"No," he screamed. "You're not real. None of this is real."

He closed his eyes to banish the sight.

"Wake up," he said to himself. "Wake up. When you open your eyes all this will be gone."

He looked again, and again he whimpered with terror.

The skull was still there.

Still there, rearing a hundred feet up out of the blackness of the plain, a vast human skull.

The impossible, the unthinkable, was still there.

And worse . . . Deep, deep in the gaping black caverns of the eye sockets . . .

SOMETHING WAS MOVING.

Chris opened his mouth and gave out a long, har-rowed, desperate scream of pure terror, before merciful nature took a hand in his agony and he fell, in a faint, facedown on the ground.

His scream was drowned by another sound. From high on the kopje, deep in a recess in the rock, a pair of old, cunning, yellow eyes looked down upon the scene.

Looked down as the man-creature, crawling now like an animal, dragged his painful way out from the fire and into the clearing, the flames from the burning fuselage glinting redly in a thousand eyes as the hyena pack swirled excitedly at the light's outer edges.

And as he watched from the blackness of the night kopje, the lion opened his mouth and once more gave out a single, shattering, thunderous territorial roar, which rippled out over the endless Serengeti night to die in echoes bouncing from kopje to plain and back to kopje.

Thirty miles away, sitting, drink in hand, in the garden of Seronera Lodge, Mike Taylor pricked up his ears.

"Hear that?" he said.

"What?" asked the American tourist.

"Lion. Long, long way off. Just caught the sound for a second on the wind."

"Oh," said the tourist. "I been watching that glow in the sky over there. What'll that be?"

"Masai fire, probably. They'll be camping out there with their cattle. Nothing to interest us."

And they both sat, safe and happily content, in the great peace of a velvet-quiet African night.

Chapter 8

A TERRIBLE SCENE WAS REVEALED BY THE DAWN.

The fires had died, but a thick, stinging smoke and a vile stench of burned metal, rubber, and oil still curled wispily up from parts of the wrecked plane and hung, flatly, like strands of ghostly gray bladder wrack in the still air. The pale dawn light slanted through the smoke, rays shifting momentarily here and there like ghouls' fingers, probing and sifting the debris scattered around the foot of the kopje.

Father and son lay huddled against a rock, clutching each other, stunned, afraid and hurt, but miraculously alive.

About fifty meters away lay the plane.

It lay on its side, its port wing rising vertical to

the sky, like a ripped, fire-blackened sail on a stranded, burned-out yacht.

In the split second before the plane had slammed into the screaming cloud of birds, the pilot had instinctively banked away. Then the screen had filled with blackness and the cockpit had imploded in a maelstrom of shattered glass, blood, bone, and feather, as one of the great, heavy vultures had come crashing through upon him. As he lost consciousness he had tried to level the plane. Too late. Still plunging, the starboard wing had rammed into the huge tattered trunk of an ancient baobab and been sliced cleanly off from the fuselage. Embedded deep into the trunk, high up in the tree, the torn and twisted metal glinted dully in the early light, a shattered knife blade in a gaping wound.

Yet this was clearly what had saved them from death. The wing hitting the tree had slewed the plane around one hundred and eighty degrees and bellyflopped it onto the ground tail first, to score a furrow a hundred yards long between tree and kopje. At one end of the furrow lay the fuselage. At the other, half buried, lay the engine, its propeller blades bent savagely outward from the block. On impact the whirling propeller had driven deep into the ground, wrenching the screaming engine away from its mountings and ripping it and the nose cone cleanly out of the plane.

Had it been otherwise, had they hit nose first, then

that same engine with its murderous propeller would have scythed back through the cockpit and cabin, shredding everything in its path like a great insane flail.

There had been another stroke of luck. The fuel tanks in the port wing had been nearly empty. The starboard had been full. When the plane finally settled on its side, with the wing rearing directly up above the fuselage, only about fifty liters of fuel had remained to seep and drip slowly down onto the cabin and its unconscious occupants. If it had been the starboard wing a thousand liters of high-octane aviation fuel could have rained down upon them. The results of the fire would have been very different then.

In fact, the fire had not started immediately. Some hours after the crash, groaning on the edge of consciousness, the pilot had stretched out an exploring arm to his left side, grounding, as he did so, several live, bared wires against an exposed piece of framework. The resulting sparks had ignited the fuel, but because there was so little of it the fire had spread slowly.

Chris's scream of terror had penetrated the darkness of his father's unconsciousness, and Mr. Harris, agonizedly dragging a limp, twisted leg, broken below the knee, had gathered the boy to him and dragged him, inch by painful inch, to the rock where they now sat.

Chris's faint had turned naturally into a deep, protective slumber, a tortured mind shutting down to give respite from the horrors around it, to give time for mind and body to adjust to the trauma.

Now the dawn had woken him, and lying quietly in his father's arms, he was able to rationalize the fearful nightmare, though the reality was hardly less fearful than the dazed dream.

The great skull of his nightmare was still there—though the dawn light revealed it for what it was, had softened its hollows and contours into a small hill of rocks and grassy ledges. But the fear of it remained. Had something moved there last night, high on the face, or was it only the horrors of imagination?

His eyes scanned the rocks and recesses anxiously. All was silent and still.

Looking now across to the blackened plane, he felt himself again shudder with fear as realization washed over him in great waves.

His escape he understood. His dazed and whirling brain had functioned at the very edges of extremity to save him from an agonizing, fiery death. It had forced his hurt and bewildered mind to drag his body out and away from danger. The boiler room, Henry's voice floating to him over vast reaches of space and time, all the confused elements of his nightmare whirling like jigsaw pieces thrown into the air by a massive hand, had fallen and slotted into place.

Except one.

The soft thud of great paws, slow and determined,

paced still, a dread muffled drumbeat in his ears. His gorge still rose as his nostrils caught the heavy stench of animal breath, blood breath, blood stench, blanketing the air in this savage and terrible place.

And that roar, that great primeval roar of triumph, reverberated still in his mind.

The jigsaw lacked one piece.

That piece was out there, quietly waiting to lock into place.

Chris stirred in his father's arms.

"Dad?"

The arms tightened reassuringly around him.

"It's all right, boy. It's all right. We're alive."

His voice was weak with pain. Chris looked up at his father's face. He was pale, his eyes dark-rimmed with shock.

"How hurt are you, Dad?" he asked.

"Not too bad. Though my leg's broken, I think. When you've gathered strength you can have a look and see what the damage is."

Chris hesitated, unwilling to forsake the security of the strong, familiar arms. He lay still for a moment, eyes swinging once more over the dreadful scene.

"Come on," he said to himself. "Come on. You have to face this. Get up."

And, drawing in breath deeply, he drew himself from the cocoon of safety and sat up. A sharp pain lanced him deep behind his left eye, and for a moment he swayed with dizziness.

"Steady, boy. You've got a bad gash."

Chris explored his forehead. A long cut ran from his temple up over his eye and into his scalp. His hair felt stiff with matted blood. The slice had missed his eye only by millimeters.

He explored further, around his head and neck, down over his rib cage, over his hips to his legs. Nothing seemed to be broken, though his hands and knees were cut, bloodied, and painful.

"OK, I'm going to try standing up," he said, and very slowly, very carefully, raised himself to a standing position.

Again a wave of dizziness, but it passed quickly.

Hesitantly he took a few steps forward, placing each foot carefully like an invalid learning to walk again. Then he turned with a weak grimace back to his father.

"Everything seems to work. Now let's look at that leg."

The leg was indeed broken. Mr. Harris screamed in agony as Chris tore back his trouser leg. Violently swollen and livid purple, the sight made Chris weak with anguish at his father's pain, but he knew as he looked at it that things could have been worse. The bone had not broken out through the flesh, so at least there was little blood loss and less risk of infection.

"It's not too bad," he said reassuringly to his father, "though we'll have to do something with it. I know how to splint breaks, if I can find some bandages and things. There must have been a first-aid kit in the plane. The pilot will know where it is . . ." He trailed off.

The pilot.

"Dad—the pilot. Where is he?"

He turned and looked out, shading his eyes now against the brilliant morning sun.

Slowly he scanned across from left to right over the clearing, over the litter of boxes and papers spewed out by the impact, over the single torn-off wheel, its twisted undercarriage embedded deep in the ground. The pilot was nowhere to be seen. Chris's eyes came to rest on the black destruction of the fuselage.

He went cold inside. Perhaps the pilot had not been as lucky as they. Perhaps he had perished there in that ugly furnace.

Perhaps he was still . . .

Chris gasped, then stopped the thought in mid-track. It was too horrific.

His father followed Chris's eyes and read his mind.

"Oh no," he whispered. "He's still in there."

"I'll go and see," said Chris, quietly.

"Don't," pleaded his father. "Look around the clearing, but don't go in the plane. If he's in there, there's nothing you can do for him. Nothing could have lived in that."

"I have to, Dad. I have to see if he's still alive. He may need help."

Whatever lay in that fuselage, he had to face it.

He had to know, had to be satisfied that he had done what needed to be done, whatever the cost to himself.

With heart full of dread he walked slowly out to the plane, afraid to his soul of what he would see.

He stopped at the tail, then walked slowly along to where the cockpit, now a yawning black hole, gazed outward and away from him like a vile, torn eye socket.

He hesitated as he approached the front of the plane. What if the pilot was still there in his seat, a brittle, charcoal effigy, staring with melted eyes out over the carnage.

Chris shuddered. Then, gathering his courage, he stepped abruptly around in front of the cockpit.

Nothing.

He sighed with a great flood of relief. The plane was empty. Smoke-blackened, charred, upholstery fire-stripped from the seat frames, foul-smelling, twisted, buckled, and hideous, it was, mercifully, empty of human horror.

Thankful, Chris stepped around and surveyed the ground behind the plane. About thirty meters away, back resting against the trunk of a small tree, lay the pilot.

Chris could see, even from that distance, that he was desperately hurt. He lay in a grotesque position, body folded, arms and legs at violent, disturbing angles, head slumped forward onto his chest, shirt shockingly red with blood.

Chris walked slowly and fearfully over to him and knelt at his side. He was still breathing, though shallowly and with a harsh, burbling sound. Blood frothed at the corners of his mouth.

Chris gently took his head into his hands and lifted it, propping it back against the tree. The man moaned softly, but the harsh rasp of his breathing quieted as the weight of his head was taken off his throat. His face was lacerated and bruised, the lips bluish under the trickle of brilliant blood.

As delicately as possible Chris began to undo the injured man's shirt. His fingers started to tremble at what he was revealing. The chest had suffered a massive blow from the side. The man was obviously terribly hurt.

Chris stood quickly and turned away. Nausea was rising up into his throat, and he had to steady himself a moment against a tree to fight it down.

Panic was rising, too.

His eyes filled with tears, and he stood for a long, long moment, breathing heavily, until the panic subsided. The situation was desperate.

He walked slowly past the tomb of the plane and sat heavily, looking at his father.

"I found him. He's very bad. His chest is crushed and he's bleeding from the mouth. Frothy blood."

"Sounds like a punctured lung. We mustn't move him if that's the case; it can be fatal."

He shifted slightly against the rock and abruptly

shouted out with pain as his shattered leg jarred with the movement.

Tears welled up again in Chris's eyes.

"Dad, what are we going to do? It's hopeless. There's only me—and I don't know what to do."

"Hold on, Chris," said his father. "Don't give way. If you give way we're sunk. I know it's terrible, but it's happened and we have to face it. Take a deep breath and let's take stock. Perhaps things aren't as bad as they appear."

Chris once more fought down the fear and hopelessness.

"All right," he said, "though I can't see how things could be worse."

"So," said Mr. Harris. "Stocktake."

"Right."

"What time is it? I've lost my watch."

"I don't know. Mine's smashed and so is the pilot's, I looked. His is stopped at five."

"Well, dawn was about half an hour ago, so it's about seven o'clock now. People at Musoma know we were due there last night, so they'll be organizing a rescue party. Yes?"

"Yes," replied Chris, "but Serengeti's a big place and no one will have any idea where we are."

"True. But they'll know approximately the route the pilot would take, so they'll search that line first."

"OK. Good," said Chris, brightening. "Except . . ."

He hesitated, not wanting to dampen the cheering thought of a rescue.

"What?"

"Except the pilot didn't fly in a straight line. He took us out to Lake Manyara and the crater."

Mr. Harris thought for a moment.

"All right, that makes it harder to find us. So they may not come today. Where does that lead us?"

"If we have to survive two or three days before we're found, we'll need food," said Chris, "and water."

"And some shelter," added his father. "Before long that sun's going to get very, very hot."

"There was some food in my bag," said Chris. "Chocolate, some fruit I bought outside the hotel while you were sleeping. Enough to stop us starving for a few days. Water, I don't know. Perhaps there was some on the plane. Or perhaps I can find some if I look around. Shelter—well, I can build something. There's all the stuff scattered around from the crash. Boxes and things."

"If you can find our cases—if they didn't get burned—there's some bed sheets. You could make us a bivouac against this rock. Anything to keep the sun off."

"Yes," said Chris, visibly cheered now.

His dad was right, as usual. Things could have been worse. Chris felt himself rising to the challenge. Perhaps there was a chance.

"Let's see what we can find."

Once more he stood and let his eyes range over the devastation, but this time with a more searching gaze. The debris was no longer the useless rags and remnants of catastrophe. Each piece had to be assessed, no matter how useless-looking, for its new potential. The burned-out fuselage would be little help, but as Chris's eyes followed the furrow from the fuselage out to the engine he could see, dotted along its edges, haphazard specks of color, the carelessly tossed remains of the plane's contents lying waiting. Out near the engine he thought he could see the blue of their suitcases, and the sight heartened him immensely.

"If I can find the bed sheets, then we've got shelter and bandages. I can see to your leg. I might even find the first-aid kit out there. Keep your fingers crossed, Dad, we're in with a chance."

And he smiled his first smile since the crash.

Chris now strode out past the plane and started to walk slowly along the furrow, eyes resting briefly on each piece of wreckage, shard of wood, scrap of cloth or metal. He kept up a running commentary as he went, calling out to his father at each new find, then placing each valuable item in the center of the furrow where he could find it on his way back. Bits of cloth for bandages, or bandannas against the sun; some thin wire for tying things; a heavy strut with a sharp jagged point where it had been torn away from the undercarriage, for digging or for a weapon; and empty plastic bottles for water if he could find some; and so on outward. Out to where the engine lay near the foot of the great baobab tree with the shining wing buried high in its trunk; out to the furrow's end, sifting, deciding, accumulating an armory of weapons against this blow that fate had dealt them. An arsenal for a war against Africa.

The area around the engine had the heaviest concentration of debris, and here Chris found the best pickings. Their suitcases, as he had thought, were there, burst open, their contents strewn but unharmed; shirts, shoes, shorts, the valuable sheets for shade, all scattered but intact.

Chris began to gather the things together. Quite suddenly he was overwhelmed with sadness as he remembered the pleasurable excitement with which, only a few hours ago, they had packed all these things, hearts thumping at the great adventure ahead.

Now look.

Their lives had been as carelessly hurled down, as meaninglessly savaged, as these poor remnants of a past life that he was unhappily collecting now. If only their lives could be put back together as easily as clothes back into a suitcase.

He pushed the last few things in and clicked down the buckled lid. Standing, he picked up the case and called as he turned back to where his father lay, out of sight, behind the stark blackness of the plane.

"Dad, I've found the . . ."

His voice trailed away into a strangled, rattling whisper in his throat. A deep wave of shock shuddered through his body. His scalp tightened, the hair rising on the back of his head. His skin crawled cold with fear, and his legs began to buckle under him.

There, ranged across the furrow, between him and the plane, between him and his father, between him and any possibility of escape or protection, was an awesome tableau.

Three full-grown lionesses sat facing him.

Motionless apart from their great tails sweeping back and forth across the grass, they surveyed him with golden, supercilious, almost bored eyes.

At their feet in stalking, hunting poses, tails threshing, mouths open in kittenish snarls, crouched their cubs.

But out beyond them, out beyond the furrow, Chris's eyes were drawn terribly, inevitably, fatefully, to the real threat.

Backward and forward on a great invisible arc paced a huge, black-maned young male. Majestic and awe-inspiring, shaking his huge head and snarling with impatience, his great feet thudded into the soft, yielding earth in a chilling, slow drumbeat.

The boy recognized him at once.

The terrible ferocity and hunger in the eyes were almost a tangible force stretching across the space between lion and boy.

The smell of blood once more hung over the clearing.

This was the nightmare.

This was him.

Chapter 9

THE OLD LION OPENED HIS EYES SLOWLY. THE MORNING light filtered deep into the depression in the rock where he lay. There was no warmth in it yet, and the night chill still stiffened his bones. He stretched, a little painfully, and grunted as his aging joints protested.

He lay still for a moment, on his side, listening to the morning sounds.

Somewhere below the cubs were playing. He could hear their mock hunting snarls and the soft growls of encouragement from the lionesses. They were learning to hunt for themselves. Already the lionesses had taught them enough to survive. They were almost fully grown, and deep inside of him the old lion's instincts were giving him unease.

Both cubs were males and soon, very soon, they would have to be driven, harshly and decisively, out of the pride, to take their predetermined places in the fragile spider's web of life on Serengeti.

Wandering over vast distances they would learn the law of Africa: The strong and the swift survive.

It was strength and speed that were failing the old lion now. Deep in his heart he knew time had outwitted him. He could no longer hunt effectively and depended now on the younger lionesses to bring down the fleet gazelle and wildebeest. The hated packs of hyenas frightened him, and he took care not to venture too far from the kopje and his territory. He needed the strength of others around him now.

The constant confrontations with the new, young outsider for control of the pride had weakened him, and he sensed that he was losing. Gradually, almost imperceptibly, the pride was slipping away from him.

The moment was close when he, too, would be driven out like the cubs. But, at the wrong end of his life, his fate would be very different from theirs.

He yawned deeply.

The night had passed uneasily. The great noise that had thundered out of the quiet, sleepy afternoon plains had shocked and frightened him and all his pride. They had scattered deep into well-used hiding places, waiting, anxious and wary, ears raised for man-sound.

In the darkening hours that had followed, he had stood guard, a lone sentinel high on the face of the kopje, watching over the strange thing that had hurled itself so cataclysmically into his domain, his territory. Watched as the upstart had padded inquisitively into the clearing and circled the huge thing, grunting and snarling around it. Watched as the first tiny flickers of flame had taken hold and grown and grown until the whole length of it had shimmered and flashed at the sky. Watched as the broken man-creatures slid like snakes or crawled like crippled hyenas away from it, away from its terrible heat and light.

Then, satisfied that these slow, pained creatures held no threat, he had slept. A troubled, anxious sleep.

Now the sounds below had changed. The light, playful snarls of the cubs were being drowned by the harsher, more urgent snarl of the outsider. He was close. Too close.

The old lion stirred, anger beginning to surge inside him. Silently he rose and padded out to the opening in the face of the rock. There below him was the pride, his pride. And with them, in his place, pacing arrogantly, carelessly in the clearing, was the hated young pretender.

White fury shot across his eyes. This was the most audacious challenge yet, and he answered it now with a great bellow of rage, a long, rippling sheet of sound that rolled from rock to rock down the kopje and out onto the clearing.

Chris's head jerked upward at the sound. From his position on his knees on the dusty ground his eyes searched the face of the rocks.

The last ten minutes had been the most terrifying and at the same time the most astonishing of his life.

As his unfinished call to his father had frozen in his throat, he had become, quite literally, paralyzed with fear. His father's anxious voice, floating from a thousand miles away, went unheeded. He could not have moved a single muscle in his body. If stillness was nature's way of fooling predators, then Chris could vouch that it didn't work. It hadn't fooled the lions.

For a while there had been little movement from the pride either, apart from their constantly threshing tails. The lionesses had sat or lain, occasionally looking away in an almost bored fashion, occasionally giving a low growl. The cubs, lying in front of them, had kept up a constant, lightly threatening barrage of snarls.

Only the big male had moved, constantly and malevolently, some distance off.

Chris had begun to feel that, if he continued to be motionless, the group might eventually just get up and go away.

He was wrong.

Quite suddenly one of the lionesses stood and,

looking directly at Chris's eyes, lowered her head and shoulders and made a violent rush straight at him. Unable even to command his eyes to close, Chris had to watch in horror as the great, supple body loped over the grass toward him, mouth opening redly, ferocious teeth bared yellow.

Even his voice was paralyzed, he found: his scream took place only in his mind.

Then, incredibly, the moment was past. At the last second the lioness had veered away, so close that he felt the rough fur brush his hand as she passed. Then, the charge over, she padded slowly, head high now, around behind him and back to her place behind the cubs. She slumped down heavily and looked out with regal disinterest over the plain.

Almost immediately one of the cubs stood. Exactly mimicking the lioness, he lowered his head almost to the ground and came at Chris with a long, low, loping stride, snarling as he came. Again, at the last second, he veered away, but not so expert as the adult, he collided heavily with Chris's legs. Chris staggered with the impact, but again froze involuntarily as he regained his balance.

Instantly the other cub came at him, veered, and passed him. He joined the first cub, and together they paced and strutted proudly back to their placcs.

So the stage was set again. The actors in this weird and savage play had taken their positions as they had been at the beginning, and waited now for scene two to commence.

Except, Chris noticed, for one.

The big male was closer, still pacing urgently back and forth, feral hatred and blood lust in his eyes.

Another lioness rose. Again the mock attack. Again the last-second swerve. Only this time as she went past, a great paw lashed carelessly out at him, knocking him sideways and winding him.

Before he had time to regain his senses the cubs were on him again. As they passed, soft paws thudded into his legs. Kitten paws, razor claws retracted. They strutted once more past, congratulating each other in low growls, returning to their places.

The lionesses purred motherly approval.

Motionless again, Chris realized that something strange and wondrous was occurring to him. The great, mind-deadening fear was lessening, and as he realized what was happening a cold, reckoning anger started to build inside him.

These lions were playing with him.

He was bait in a hunting lesson. That was how significant he was here. Something to be swatted and tapped, intimidated and terrorized, humiliated and exterminated. An ant crushed underfoot.

Well, he wasn't going to die whimpering and squeaking like some mouse being patted to death by a cat. He would fight. Face savagery with savagery.

Survive!

Suddenly he found he could move again.

Desperately his eyes searched along the furrow. Exactly where he had left it, about halfway between himself and the pride, lay the heavy, sharp-pointed piece of undercarriage that he had marked for a weapon.

"All right," he said, "if you're going to play the life out of me, at least I'm going to take one of you with me."

Coldly furious now, he looked directly at the pride. The long-hidden savage who exists within all of us was rising.

Without giving himself time to think, he began to run at top speed straight toward the pride. And as he ran he screamed a great cry of battle, a cry from the depths of his being, a cry uttered by countless millions of cornered and harrowed creatures stretching back to the dawn of time before him.

The result was electrifying.

So sudden, so unexpected was the charge that the lionesses and cubs were momentarily shocked and startled. Leaping up, they began to back away, snarling in confusion.

Even the big male stopped his pacing and stood, unsure.

This brief reversal of attacker and attacked gave Chris the time he needed to reach the metal spar. Thudding to his knees beside it, he quickly swept it up into his hands, brandishing the vicious, jaggedly broken point at the milling pride.

For a moment they were impressed and moved uneasily about.

But not for long.

The uneasy, uncertain movements gradually took on a pattern as each of the lionesses began to slide into her well-remembered position. One remained in the center of the furrow; the other two began to fan out to the sides. The big male, now out to Chris's right, began a long, slow arc, heading around to get behind him. The cubs snarled excitedly and chased in and out of the lionesses' legs before settling on paths of their own.

The atmosphere had changed.

The eyes had changed.

This was no longer a game. These were the steady, confident maneuvers of the kill.

The air was now charged with death. In the liquid golden eyes, in the wet salivating redness of the open jaws, in the silky, rippling flow of supple muscles, in the dead-march thump, thump, thump of heavy paws.

Chris knew that it was the end. Yet the calm anger remained. He was determined that death would not find him cringing and whimpering.

Slowly he turned his back on the advancing lionesses.

The great male of his nightmare had completed his arc and stood now, very still, watching the boy.

Boy's eyes met lion's, both reading deep into the other.

"Come on, then," whispered Chris. "You. I'll take you."

He braced the weapon against the ground.

And the lion began to move.

Erect, head high, contemptuously slowly . . . the lion began to move.

The circle was complete.

From six points, lithe golden death contracted relentlessly down onto the small, hopeless dot at its center, when, from high on the face of the kopje came a great bellow of rage, a long rippling sheet of sound that rolled from rock to rock down the kopje and out onto the clearing.

Chapter 10

IT DIDN'T TAKE MUCH TO MAKE MIKE TAYLOR A HAPPY man. Heaven, for him, was grinding slowly along in four-wheel drive, heat hammering through the roof of the cab, a Land Rover engine singing sweetly.

So he was happy now, peering through the dust-coated windshield, trying to follow the almost invisible, overgrown track through the scrubby bush.

Ten miles back they had turned off the long red ribbon of dirt road that snakes up through Serengeti to the Kenyan border, onto this little-known, ancient track heading east to Lake Natron.

This was Mike's element. Wild, unknown, unpopulated, unfrequented. Out here in the harsh scrubland of Africa, he was in his place. A strange, emaciated anachronism in a town, out here he fitted.

His precious tourist, Hyram T. Johnson, was a

little happier now, too. The day had not started well for him. Africa had not been very obliging. Up before dawn, hunched with the weight of expensive Zeiss binoculars and a Nikon camera hanging around his neck, he had waited and watched for the great pageant of life to begin. The dawn light had gradually come up over the water hole, and the camera, with its massive ugly lens, had been poised.

The shutter had remained closed.

Nothing had moved out on the lightening plains. Nothing at all.

Hyram had been furious. Serengeti was full of animals. He knew that. Didn't every television program he had ever seen about Africa show the plains to be teeming with zebra, giraffe, gazelle, lion, and elephant? Where were they? Where were the elephants?

"Where are the elephants?" he demanded of Mike, who appeared, bleary with sleep, in the hotel dining room an hour later.

"What?" he asked, incredulously, slumping down at the table and waving to a waiter.

"The elephants. Where are the goddamn elephants? You said there'd be elephants at Seronera. I been here since dawn watching. Not a thing. Not a goddamn thing. I come ten thousand miles to photograph trees?"

Mike stared, open-mouthed, hardly believing what he was being asked.

In a way he pitied him, this loud, self-important man from another world. A world where everything obeyed his whim. What did he think? Pick up a telephone and order elephants like ordering a pizza? Flick a switch and turn Africa on? Photograph it and turn it off again?

"I didn't exactly mean here at the hotel, though sometimes they pass and call at the water hole. They'll be close. Some big herds were sighted last week moving southwest toward the crater. If you want elephants, I'll find you elephants."

"Yeah, I want them all right," said Hyram. "What's your plan?"

"If they're moving southwest they're going into very remote country. Just north of here there's an old Masai herding track that runs across country to Natron. We could follow that for a way, then take to the bush and head south. It'll be very rough and very slow. We'll have to camp overnight, then tomorrow we can join the road again and head back here."

"Camp?" There was alarm in Hyram's voice. "Is that safe?"

"Safer than Central Park," replied Mike.

"Yeah? Don't knock Central Park. I seen more animals in Central Park than I seen here."

A moment later he added, "Mostly there they got two legs, though."

So the plan had been set, and now Mike was humming quietly as Bennie trundled the big dependable Land Rover along, a great cloud of red dust blowing up behind it to hang glinting and flashing in the bright morning sun. The country here was scrubby, with thick, fiercely sharp thornbushes matting the land and growing out onto the disused track.

"Just a bit farther along here," said Mike, "and the country opens out. We'll leave the track then and head south."

"Who'll know the difference?" said the perspiring American from the backseat. "I ain't seen no track for an hour. All I seen is bushes and dust."

Mike smiled to himself. He often regretted that his living depended on entertaining people like this, and he was getting some small, perverse satisfaction at the man's discomfort.

"We come out onto open grassland in a minute. Then we'll set about finding you your elephants."

They were down in bottom gear now, climbing a long, gentle slope up through the dense thorns. As the Land Rover pushed relentlessly through them, they scraped long, nerve-grating screeches down its length. Foot barely pressing the accelerator, Bennie let the big machine pull itself gradually up to the top of the slope.

They came over the rise and stopped.

The scrubland sloped gradually away from them down to a lazy, muddy-brown river flowing quietly southward. Beyond, a great, lonely plain stretched away and away until it merged, misty blue, with the cloudless sky far, far in the distance.

There was a stunned silence in the Land Rover.

The quiet tick of the engine died away as Bennie turned the key.

What luck. What incredible luck.

Quite by chance they had stumbled on one of the most awe-inspiring sights that Africa has to offer.

Silently, one by one, they got out of the Land Rover and climbed up onto its roof and hood. Even the loud tourist had lost his voice.

The plain below them was covered with an immense mass of slowly moving dark dots.

A shifting sea of wildebeest. A deluge, a flood of these strange, gentle creatures, blanketed the bright green expanse. A vast mosaic of quietly grazing gray and black shapes. A countless, unimaginable number. Half a million? A million? Who could begin to guess?

And still they came.

Radiating in long, flowing threads of black, out to the very edges of sight, rivers of them wound and flowed inward to swell the great, eerie lake of beasts. Relentless and inexorable living rivers, driven by some dimly felt, ancient and inescapable urge, unfathomable by man.

From the vast distances of the shimmering horizons a single, mystic grail of thought was drawing them here to this place.

"My God," said the American, very quietly. "I asked for animals. So now I got animals."

"Yes," said Mike. "Now you got animals."

"What?" asked Hyram. "What is it? What brings them here?" He spoke very softly, like a man in church.

"It's very simple," said Mike. "At least, one explanation is. The short rains round about Christmastime make the grass grow and fill the water holes. There's a lot of calcium in the grass now, and in the water. That's what they come for."

There was a long silence as they all drank deeply of the spectacle before them.

"No," said the American at length, "that's not it. That's not what brings them."

"That's what the scientists say."

"Scientists, schmientists," he snorted. "What do they know with their notebooks and their calculators? You wanna know what makes life tick, ask a poet, not a scientist."

Mike looked at him with growing respect.

"I don't know any poets. We don't get many coming this way. But you're right. There are some things we can't explain. We're looking at one of them."

They grinned at each other, a sudden understanding, a kinship established.

For a long, long time they stood under the great, blue vault of sky, each with his own thoughts, each drawing from this huge, majestic tapestry his own wonderment, his own search for meaning.

"So," said Mike, eventually, "shall we go and find your elephants?"

Hyram nodded and they all began to move, climbing down from the Land Rover.

At the door, the American stopped, giving a long, last look down onto the plain. He shook his head in disbelief.

"Calcium, eh?"

He spat contemptuously.

"Goddamn calcium."

For a while they drove on in silence, deeply affected by what they had seen. Heading south now, they followed the long line of the hill, keeping the plain and the wildebeest to their left. Then, when they judged that they would not disturb the peacefully grazing herd, they dropped down and out onto the flat green grass of the plain.

The going now became easier, and Bennie set the Land Rover bouncing and thumping cheerfully along, dodging rocks and bushes.

"*Tembo* country soon, bwana," he said, pointing out into the distance ahead.

Mike followed his pointing finger and nodded.

"What's that?" asked Hyram.

"Baobab trees. Find a baobab and you stand a good chance of finding an elephant. They love the bark. They'll happily rip a baobab to shreds with their tusks."

Hardly had he finished the sentence than he was thrown violently forward as Bennie stamped hard on the brake.

The Land Rover lurched to a very abrupt halt.

"Bennie, what on earth?"

The driver looked at Mike with a puzzled expression. He put the vehicle into reverse and backed slowly, watching the ground from the side window as they went. Finally he pulled up.

"Bwana, come," he said, climbing out of the Land Rover.

Mike followed him to the front. Bennie pointed at the grass. In a muddy depression in the ground was a very clear imprint of a large tire. A Land Rover or truck tire.

"So? Is that any reason to fling me headfirst through the windshield?"

"Bwana, nobody comes here, you know that. The safari companies don't venture this side. And that mark is fresh."

"So, what are you telling me?" asked Mike, though he knew what he was being told.

"Find a baobab, find an elephant. Find an elephant . . ." He shrugged and let Mike finish the sentence for himself.

"Poachers," said Mike tightly.

"Bwana, we turn back now. These men are dangerous."

"Turn back? I've never turned away from a poacher in my life. I'm not starting now."

"Bwana, please. I have a friend, a guide in Ngorongoro. He says now these men are dangerous. Now they do not hunt with rifles. Now they have machine guns. Please, bwana, we go back."

"We go on," said Mike, his voice heavy with determination.

He walked quickly back to the Land Rover. Opening the back door, he drew from its leather case the long hunting rifle with the telescopic sight. Reaching into a canvas bag, he broke open a box of the heavy three-inch shells and dropped half a dozen into the pocket of his shirt. Then he returned to the passenger seat and climbed in.

"Drive on," he said to Bennie, "and keep your eyes peeled."

"You bet, bwana," replied Bennie, unhappily.

"What's going on?" asked Hyram. "What's that for?"

"Just a precaution. Your precious elephants, if we find them, might not be too pleased to see us. They're the most dangerous things around here." And he added "almost" under his breath.

The Land Rover ground slowly on toward the line of trees, the land now beginning to slope gently upward again. About half a mile from the trees he told Bennie to stop.

"Switch off," he said. And taking the binoculars, he climbed up over the hood to stand on the roof rack, scanning carefully from left to right.

A thin gray wisp of smoke curled upward behind the trees and, very faintly on the air, he could hear voices. Behind the voices a steady clack, clack, clack.

Bennie had been right. Mike felt sick. He knew what that sound was. He dropped lightly down from the roof.

"Load the other gun, Bennie. You stay and look after things here. I've got a small job to do."

He reached into the cab, drew out the gun, and set off with a long, easy stride in the direction of the line of trees.

"Be careful, bwana," called Bennie. But already Mike was melting into the bush.

Moving easily, taking advantage of trees and thornbushes, he made his way toward the top of the rise. His face was set hard with anger. This moment he had lived many times before, in Selous, as the great locust plague of ivory poaching had gained ground. Man sickened him at these times. Not just the hard, desperate men he knew he was going to find here at their vile and savage trade, but also the faceless ones who made it possible. The simpering women with the dead-white necklaces around their throats, the countless suburbanites standing ivory carvings on sideboards a world away from Africa. Would they buy it if they had to pull the trigger; if they had to watch this most wonderful and strange of earth's inhabitants crash, bloodied and twitching, in death throes to the dust? Would they take up the ax and hack away the ivory from the still-warm flesh of the elephant's great head?

Cold-faced, he clicked the heavy bullets into the

gun as he crept the last few yards to the top of the hill.

The voices were loud now, and he went down on his knees and crawled silently until he could look over the rise. He stopped and sat behind a rock for a minute, taking control of himself. Experience had taught him that anger was an enemy.

Then he rose, moved out to the side, and surfaced over the crest of the hill.

Cool now as a machine, analytically, surgically, he took stock.

A fire. A spit with a large piece of meat roasting. Two men sat by the fire. A Land Rover—dark green, canvas back. Huge white tusks protruding beyond the canvas; one, two, three pairs.

Fury began to rise.

Keep it down. Keep the fury down.

Elephant, lying on the ground.

His eyes flicked from one great carcass to another. Two on their sides, another lying upright, its legs collapsed beneath it. Shocking, terrible holes of blood where the tusks had been axed out of their skulls.

A fourth elephant. Another man, very tall, Somali, ax still raised, still in the act of hacking at this great, noble, quiet creature.

All right. Let go!

Now you can let go!

The gun rose as his fury rose. The men's positions clear in his mind now. He could afford his anger.

Bang! The first shot went away, the recoil thudding into his shoulder. The raised ax arced away as the bullet hammered into the Somali's arm. He screamed, spun with the impact, and fell writhing to the ground.

Rifle still at his shoulder, Mike tracked the barrel and sight smoothly across to the other two men. They had jumped to their feet and stood poised, like long, black birds about to take flight.

Bang! The second. A spurt of dust shot up a few feet behind the two men. Missed.

The moment of shocked confusion over, the two men began to run toward the Land Rover.

Bang! Three. The lead man spun in midstep, one leg knocked from under him by the heavy bullet. The second man raced past him.

Bang! Four. A long zinging as the bullet hit the tailgate of the vehicle and went spinning uselessly away into the bush.

Now, careful. Two bullets left. The barrel panned once more back to the first man. He lay still. No threat.

Back again to the right. No sign of either man. They had gained the shelter of the Land Rover.

Suddenly the starter motor whirred and the engine fired. They had climbed in from the passenger side. Rapidly the vehicle backed, erratically swaying from side to side, across to the injured man. It came to a halt, blocking Mike's sight of him.

Damn! He couldn't see any of them.

Wait now.

Take hold again.

What now? Two bullets left.

Shoot out the tires?

Then what?

An empty gun and I'm easy prey for them.

Slowly, regretfully, he let the barrel of the gun fall.

The engine revved, and the Land Rover shot away across the clearing, out through the trees, and went careering and bouncing, the great ivory tusks clattering in the back, away to the west.

Mike sighed heavily.

He stood for a long, anguished moment watching the vehicle go.

"There'll be another time," said a quiet voice behind him.

Mike spun around to find Hyram Johnson only a few feet away from him. The man's face was hard with rage and shock.

"Yes," said Mike, heavily, "there's always another time."

Then, as his eyes turned back to the great, gray, tragic beasts, their bloody masks silently echoing their death agony, he sent the final two bullets winging uselessly, in savage anger, after the Land Rover.

A few miles to the west the distant gunshots floated, very faint but unmistakable, into the clearing where a great and savage drama was taking place.

Chapter 11

THE DEADLY CIRCLE HAD STOPPED CONTRACTING. Hardly breathing, Chris watched in awed fascination.

Standing now on a ledge near the summit of the kopje, a clear gold silhouette against the pale rock, the old lion raised his huge, scarred head and roared at the sky.

It was not so much a sound as a force. Elemental, like a rolling thunderclap that shuddered the air, that battered in waves outward and thudded, like blows to the chest, into Chris's body.

With confused eyes the lionesses and cubs had begun to back off. Slinking, heads lowered like the sly hyenas, they looked ashamed, abashed.

Another roar, demanding, imperious, and they were all on the move, answering the command.

Slowly, weaving in and out around each other, they slid back toward the foot of the kopje, their low, snarling growls of disappointment and protest fading to silence.

Silence.

Chris turned his head back to face the young lion. He had not moved. But now his head was turned upward. He was uncertain and wary, the patriarch's defiant challenge having driven Chris from his mind.

The boy remained motionless, makeshift spear still angled in readiness, shaft driven into the soft soil, point ready.

Suddenly the young lion, too, was on the move. Turning away from Chris, he started to pace, first outward, away from the kopje, then ranging in an arc, padding a long curve out toward the open plain, then swinging back to complete a circle. Then round again, pad, pad, pad, feet stamping out the degrees of the circle, swinging away and back in great arcs. As he went his massive head swung from side to side, and with each measured beat of his paws he gave a heavy, guttural snarl. A deep, low thunder from the pit of his stomach, rhythmical and infinitely menacing.

Pad. *Rrrrr*. Pad. *Rrrrr*. Pad. *Rrrrr*.

Desperately slowly Chris began to rise. He knew now that, for a time at least, he was forgotten. An age-old saga was being played out before him. The majestic beast was treading out his battleground, and Chris, a tiny, insignificant ant, could withdraw.

He stood and began to back away, one slow, cautious foot at a time. Left. Pause. Right. Pause. Left. Gradually widening the gap between himself and the circling, snarling beast. Then abruptly, he spun on his heels, breaking out of the spin into a headlong, hurtling dash back down the empty scar of ground to drop, breathless, into the shadow of the plane.

His father called out in relief as Chris came into sight again.

"Chris. Thank God. I couldn't see you for the plane. I thought . . ."

"It's all right, Dad. I'm OK. I'll tell you about it in a minute. Just wait. We're safe for the moment."

The lionesses and cubs had reached the kopje and were rising gradually in deliberate, slow bounds up the rocks, pausing now to look at the young lion below, now at their growling sovereign above. As they approached the summit their shoulders fell lower until they almost crawled, apologetic and cringing. Finally they draped themselves in a group a few feet below the old lion.

His pride back in its rightful place, the old lion began to descend, still giving small growls of admonishment for their behavior. Slow and watchful, his yellow eyes fixed on his adversary, he approached the flat ground, finally thudding down onto the grass to stand motionless and silent, head thrust forward, tail swinging slowly from side to side. The young lion stopped his provocative pacing and faced him.

From the kopje the lionesses and cubs watched,

very still, but with vigilant, calculating eyes. The scene reminded Chris for all the world of a Roman coliseum. The crowd looking on, assessing the chances of the combatants. The gladiators appraising each other across the arena. "We who are about to die salute thee." The difference, the dread, appalling difference, was that those conflicts of old had no consequence for the watchers. Whoever lived or died in those terrible, bloodstained fighting pits of history, the shouting crowds simply got up and went home. Here things were very different.

The events of the last hour had made the nature of this strange and massive confrontation very clear to Chris. Now, as he looked at the old lion, he could see that the impressive and majestic bearing could not conceal the thinness and the sunken flesh of age. On the kopje the sunlight had sheened this animal with gold, and distance had made him an enchanted statue, a shining thing of power and majestic command. Close to, Chris realized with a sinking heart, the gold coat faded to a dull threadbare khaki rug hung in loose folds on a stiff and protruding clotheshorse of bones.

How could he be a match for that awesome malevolence waiting out there in the center of that invisibly imprinted battleground?

Yet there was nothing uncertain about his bearing or his eyes; both still carried the stamp of a veteran warrior. And, as he began to move out to do battle, there was no fear, no doubt, in his stately, strutting walk. Chris was afraid for him, but obviously the lion had no fear for himself.

Almost carelessly he paced out from the foot of the kopje and passed the ruined hulk of the plane within ten feet of where Chris knelt in the shadow cast by the wing. So close, the heavy smell of the animal burned like acrid smoke in Chris's nostrils.

Then he was past and padding out to face the challenger, increasing speed as he approached. The careless saunter became a determined trotting motion, head and shoulders rising, then a canter, then finally the great bounding gallop of a predator in full chase. There was no subtlety in this attack, no tactics or cunning strategies, circlings or subterfuges. Just five hundred pounds of balled single-minded ferocity crashing across the ground. And as he went the snarling began. Deep, resonant snarls of rage and hatred booming out of the prehistoric mists of time, crashing back to echo from the kopje face.

The hurtling charge ended with a muffled, dead thud of flesh, a thump that made Chris gasp, as the two lions came together. It was a crash that felled the young lion and sent him spinning head over heels in the dust. He recovered, rolling into a sitting position; thrust back on his haunches, with one huge paw raised lashing at the air, lips drawn back in a spitting snarl of anger. Instantly the old lion was on him, ignoring the terrible, raking claws, diving forward, jaws seeking throat.

Again they came together, lashing and snapping,

and locked, rolling from side to side, in a lurching, threshing ball of spitting fury, each great-toothed mouth trying to batten onto the other's throat in the final strangling of the kill.

Chris watched, heart thumping, as the battle raged back and forth. It was impossible to tell which lion held the advantage, impossible even, in the confused rolling and thrashing, to know which lion was which.

Then the ball broke as one lion rolled out in a sideways spin and jumped to his feet. It was the younger, more agile lion who had escaped. Spinning quickly, he reared up on his hind legs, both paws lashing at the older lion's back end. Slower to recover, the older lion was caught by the heavy blows to his haunches. Vicious claws ripped the loosely hanging skin, exposing raw red flesh, and the impact spun his back legs around from under him. Taking advantage of the spin, he rose up underneath the flailing paws and fastened his jaws on the young lion's throat.

He had him.

The jaws closed like a vise. For a second they froze, the young lion still raised up on his back legs but suspended now by his throat. Then, with a swift, vicious sideways twist of the head the old lion hurled him onto his back where he lay struggling, his legs uselessly windmilling in the air, snarls turning to choking gasps as giant pincers closed upon his windpipe.

Chris willed the old lion to hold on. Somewhere

deep in his instincts he knew that his own survival and the survival of the injured men behind him was inextricably bound up with this brief, titanic struggle now moving to its close. For the first time in his life he was willing something else to die.

"Hold on," he called with his mind. "Hold."

But it was not to be.

Floating in from the plains, faint but clear and unmistakable, came the high crack of a rifle shot.

Chris's head whipped around and up at the sound.

The lions froze into statues, still locked at mouth and throat.

Crack! A second shot rolling in on the smooth basin of the sky.

All thought of conflict driven from their minds now by a single common fear, the pair broke up. The old lion, releasing his grip, stepped back and turned anxiously toward the sound. Here lay a much greater danger, a danger he knew well and was more afraid of than any other.

Crack!

The young lion had already leaped to his feet. He paused uncertainly for a second, looking first outward at the rifle sound, then back to his alert, watchful adversary.

Crack! A fourth shot.

They both made their moves. The young lion set off on a long lope outward, away from the clearing, away from the battleground, swinging west, away from the direction of the gun. The old lion watched him go, then turning back, he listened for a moment, head on one side to catch the sounds. Then he swung around and began to make his way back to the kopje.

The fight had taken its toll. The old warrior limped painfully, and Chris could see the long tears in his haunches where the claws had ripped open the skin. His heart went out to him. Fate had again played a trick, had snatched a victory from this old, unsteady creature. True, he had driven the challenger off—this time. But now there would be a next time. And the victor looked defeated. Back legs dragging, breathing heavily, he now looked older than before; a sad, hurt old animal lamely hobbling back to safety.

As the lion approached, Chris rose, strangely, inexplicably unafraid. The lion continued his painful path, passing Chris at the same point as he had passed earlier. Without breaking his step he turned his great, old, weary head toward the motionless boy.

For the briefest of moments their eyes met. As the split-second click of a camera shutter captures and freezes a tiny tick of time, so a picture flashed across from eye to eye. Momentarily, two vastly different creatures, each storm-driven and harried in his separate circumstances, touched minds as they read the eyes of one another.

Each read the same things. Dismay, anxiety, the deep bewilderment of creatures caught up in forces

101

they were unable to control. Forces that were near to defeating them. Each read fear in the eyes of the other.

Then the moment was gone. With a soft snarl the lion drew a veil over his eyes and continued his steady plod back toward the kopje.

Chris watched him go, startled and deeply disturbed by this fleeting glimpse into another, stranger life. Through the window of those time-worn yellow eyes he had seen doubt. Instinct was telling him now that doubt lay only one step in front of death. Neither he nor this old, tired animal could afford doubt.

The lion began to climb the kopje, grunting with effort as he leaped his way upward from boulder to boulder. As he passed the watchful lionesses and cubs, it seemed to Chris that he drew himself up a little for their benefit. His lips curled back in a last snarl of rebuke, then he made the final leap up to the high cleft that led down into his cool, dim sanctuary.

At the entrance he paused and turned his head outward to scan the plain.

Chris held his breath.

From below, distance took the years and the hurts away from the old beast, and silhouetted once again against the gray rocks, he seemed renewed. He was gold power, awesome and strong again, eyes burning from his great, black-maned head, searching the shifting heat for his adversary.

There was a long silence.

"Go on," Chris whispered in his mind, willing the thought across the still, heat-laden air. "Roar."

The lion remained silent and motionless.

"Go on," whispered Chris, more urgently. "Don't doubt. Tell him—like you did before. Tell him you're still king."

He sent the thought singing out over the space between them, desperate to reach through those doubting eyes to the animal's heart. To *give* the animal heart.

"Roar," he called with his mind.

But there was only silence; silence and deadening heat, as the great head lowered and the lion turned wearily and dropped, without sound, into the black gash in the rock.

Chris's shoulders slumped with disappointment, and tears sprang abruptly to his eyes.

"No," he whispered, "don't. Don't give up. We'll beat him. We have to beat him."

He turned his face out toward the shimmering plain, screwing his eyes up against the blinding glare. Heat was floating the trees in a white lake of light.

Somewhere out there, raging and menacing, the threat remained.

"We'll beat you," he said. "I'm not going to give up. I'm going to live. I'm going to get us out of here. Somehow I am going to get us out of here."

He turned and started to walk slowly back to where

his father lay. He was already beginning to plan the things he had to do.

As he walked, two more shots, very faint and very far, floated in quick succession from the eastern plain.

Chapter 12

IT WAS AFTERNOON.

They lay in the makeshift bivouac Chris had rigged against the rock—a sheet held up at the front by broken branches that he had picked up from the foot of the tree and tied together with wire ripped out of the plane. At the back the sheet rested on the rock and was weighed down with stones. This tiny protection gave them a feeling of security out of all proportion to its flimsiness.

Noon had passed in a white blaze. Throughout the morning Chris had watched the shadow cast by the plane's wing gradually shorten until it had disappeared. Now it was beginning to emerge on the other side. He had laid two sticks on the ground in the form of a compass cross and placed a small stone at the end of the arm he guessed pointed due north. He would be able to confirm his guess at sunset.

Dad was still sleeping. Together they had tended to his leg. A shattered wooden box had yielded two suitable lengths of wood, and a torn-up sheet had made the bindings. With shaking hands Chris had, with one decisive movement, pushed down onto the break, pressing the broken bone ends as close together as possible, then bound the wood to the front and back of the leg to keep it straight. His dad had screamed with the pain of it but had remained conscious. As the pain had settled to a steady throb he had fallen into a quiet, recuperative sleep.

The pilot had remained unconscious. Chris had made him as comfortable as possible, draping a sheet over the branches of the tree he lay against and resting his head on a pillow of clothes. There was little more he could do for him than that.

It had been a nervous and watchful morning, eyes drawn again and again to the kopje, out to the plain and back to the kopje.

But the lions had ignored them. The old male had disappeared into his cave and had not emerged again. The lionesses and cubs had slept all morning. There had been no sign of the young male since the shots had sent him swinging away and out onto the plain.

Yet, even though they seemed oblivious to the human intruders, the lions' presence hung on the air like a thick, damp fog of foreboding. Every intake of breath tasted of lion. Every movement, every thought was dominated, dictated even, by their proximity. Chris sensed that, even with their terrible, golden eyes closed in sleep, they knew exactly where he was, knew every move as soon as he made it. Lions don't need eyes; they see with every nerve of their bodies.

An occasional animal had ventured close. A pair of inquisitive zebra had stood, sniffing the air, a few yards out beyond the baobab. Chris had stood to look out past them, searching the plain for the young lion, and they had started, whirled in fright, and galloped off, their hooves raising tiny whirlwinds of dust, the air filled momentarily with hollow drums of sound. In the heat of midmorning, mirage had swallowed them, turning them to striped paint splodges bobbing silently at the edge of a vast pale sea. At noon, a lone hyena, greed overcoming fear, had paced the perimeter of the clearing, then made a mad dash inward to snatch up one of the broken, twisted bundles of feathers littered around the plane. Trying to scurry away with his parcel of carrion, he had tripped and stumbled over the awkward, floppy corpse, chattering his irritation as he pulled and tugged it away. A comic, ridiculous sight that in better times would have brought a laugh to Chris's lips.

Apart from these, and a tiny Thomson's gazelle who had tiptoed past them, delicate and poised, the day had been almost silent; a burning, heavy silence broken only by a distant bark or bellow beyond sight out on the plain, or the leathery slap of vulture wings as a lone scout passed on his eternal, grave-robbing search.

Chris found himself hating these vile and ugly birds, circling high in the blue vault, resolute and single-minded in the quest for death. Yet in a strange way the hatred gave him strength. To perish here was unthinkable; to die watched by a circle of cold, viciously patient eyes; to die knowing that those terrible curved beaks waited to pierce and pull and tear your still-warm flesh; just the thought brought a fierce rage of determination flooding up to Chris's throat.

"Wait all you like," he had said to the sky. "You won't get me."

He hadn't spoken of his plan yet to his father. Throughout the morning they had listened hopefully for the drone of a search plane or the twanging clatter of a helicopter. They had heard nothing.

A hundred times Chris had shaded his eyes with his hands and searched the great flatness of the plain for vehicles, or people, or smoke, or any sign of human life. There had been none.

The faint hope that the distant gunshots would be repeated closer, or that human voices or the hum of a motor would drift in to them had faded with the ticking of the hours.

But hope was not gone. Far from it.

Moving quietly about the area, collecting up the scattered, tattered pieces of another world, Chris had felt his resolution firming as his plan took shape. Each small success had given him further strength. And there had been many successes. He had found water, twenty liters of it, in a fire-blackened jerrican at the rear end of the plane. Beside it had been a metal toolbox, wondrously, heart-stoppingly, containing an ax and a machete among the tools. He had found his bag with the food he had saved for the flight and the fruit he had bought outside the hotel. Survival and escape was no longer just an instinctive, animal will to live, as it had been before. It had become, as the morning progressed, a clear, itemized campaign in Chris's mind; a campaign any primitive man would have recognized, in a world where life was stripped down to the elemental necessities of all men in all times: food, water, shelter. Such had been Chris's search. In a small way he had tamed his world, as countless millions before him had done. Had sifted and sorted until, for today at least, there was shelter from the killing sun, food to eat, and water to drink.

And because of those things there was hope. There was future.

He glanced out at the shadow cast by the wing, then at his makeshift compass on the ground. A correct bearing would be vital to his plan.

The sun was still quite high, and he guessed it would be about one o'clock. Later, when the sun was less fierce, he would walk out to the trees and collect wood for a fire. If he could keep it burning through-out the night they should be safe from the predators. His eyes were once more drawn out to the plain.

I wonder what he's doing, he thought. *Licking his hurt dignity? Plotting what to do next with us?*

"What are you thinking, son?" His dad had woken and had been watching him.

"Hi, Dad. How do you feel?"

"I'm all right. The leg's throbbing a lot, but I'm OK."

"I was just wondering where that lion was."

"Perhaps he's gone for good," ventured his father.

Chris knew there was no hope of that. Dad hadn't seen his eyes, hadn't seen the terrible longing, the desperate craving for blood that had burned in scorching waves out from those golden pools of hate. No, he was out there yet, waiting. And he was angry. Chris could feel the anger seeping over the ground from the plain to squat toadlike over them.

"No, Dad, he's there," he said simply. "I know he's there."

"What about the others on the rock?" Mr. Harris groaned as he shifted his position.

Chris's eyes moved upward to scan the kopje.

"Same as before. No one's moved."

He snapped back the spout lid on the jerrican and poured a little water into the plastic bottle he had found earlier. He gave it to his father.

"Dad, I've got to talk to you now about what I'm going to do."

"All right, let's hear it."

"I've been thinking all morning about what's happened and what I can do, and I've come to some conclusions. I took the pilot some water while you were asleep. He hasn't regained consciousness, but I washed his face and trickled some water into his mouth. I think he swallowed some, but he's in a very bad way. Unless he has help soon, he'll die, I'm sure of it. Even though we have food and water and could afford to sit and wait for a rescue party, he can't. And something else won't wait. That lion out there —he won't wait. Tomorrow or the next day he'll be back. And next time there may be nothing to stop him."

"I don't know what you're getting at. How can we do anything but wait?"

"Well, I've figured some things out, Dad. These are the things I know. When we came out of Ngorongoro Crater the pilot set a course northwest—I saw him do it. Then, when we talked about Mike Taylor, he said we would pass over Seronera Lodge in about half an hour."

"All right, I'm keeping up, just," said Mr. Harris.

"Right. The next bit's guesswork and logic combined. Say we were traveling at a hundred and twenty miles an hour—half an hour's flying would make it sixty miles from the crater to the lodge. Now, I don't know how long we flew before we crashed, but if we guess at fifteen minutes we would have traveled thirty miles. So there you are."

"Where?"

"Seronera Lodge is about thirty miles northwest of us. At sunset I'll be able to pinpoint northwest exactly."

"Then what?"

"Dad, walking and running I can cover thirty miles in five or six hours. If I leave here at dawn I'll find the lodge by noon and have help back here for you both sometime in the afternoon."

His father's mouth fell open in shock.

"What? Walk? In this country? Are you crazy? Chris, I forbid it. Absolutely, totally forbid it."

"I knew you would. But there's no other way, Dad. I can't sit here and watch that man die when I'm perfectly capable of doing that distance. And anyway, the pilot said something else. When I asked him whether we would see Mike Taylor on the road he said we would follow the road for a little way before we got to Seronera. So I might find the road, and perhaps people, in less miles than we think."

Mr. Harris's face had gone pale.

"Chris, this is Africa. You don't stand a chance."

"I do, Dad. Don't ask me how I know that, but I do know it. I know it's dangerous, but something inside me tells me it's right and it's possible. And I'm going to do it. I have to."

There was a long pause as Mr. Harris studied his son's face anxiously.

"I see," he said eventually. "I can tell by your expression that there's no point in my arguing."

"No point at all, Dad. You didn't know your son was so stubborn, did you?"

"I think I didn't know my son at all," said Mr. Harris, quietly. "It's a great privilege to get to know him now."

"So, that's settled, then," said Chris. "Now I'm going to go and chop some wood."

"What? Chop wood? Can you manage with those sore hands?"

"They're OK. Tonight we'll have a fire all night to keep the animals away. I'll chop enough for tomorrow, too—you'll be able to keep it going. Who knows, somebody may see the smoke."

Picking up the ax, Chris walked out across the clearing and toward the trees. Several branches lay at the foot of the baobab. He would start there. He moved slowly and quietly, anxious not to antagonize the lionesses. But they ignored him, remaining in their indolently draped poses on the rocks. Flicking his eyes constantly to left and right, he watched the plain for movement as he approached the tree. The impact of the wing had sent a shower of tattered bark and branches dropping down to the ground. Enough wood for a couple of days at least. He gave a last, long and careful search with his eyes. There was no sign at all of the young lion. Far, far out a long ribbon of wildebeest drew a fine black line between green earth and blue sky—a long pencil line of slow-moving life in the vast emptiness and silence.

Then the silence was broken by the steady thud of

the ax as Chris set about the task of cutting the life-preserving wood. Methodically hacking the branches into manageable lengths, he tried to rationalize his fear. Inside he was not as confident as the outer face he had presented to his father. The dangers were enormous and daunting, but they were no less so if he remained here. In fact, if he could get away quietly without the lionesses or the young male out on the plain seeing him, the dangers might even be less out there than here. He was young and fit and he could run like the wind. And he had to go. Two men's lives depended upon him.

Behind him, as he chopped at the sweet-smelling wood, in the silence of distance, the horizon was changing shape. The great black line of wildebeest was beginning to break. Black, shaggy heads had turned; watchful eyes and ears had picked up a strange, dark, humming shape approaching them from the east. Mothers called to calves to rejoin them; anxious bulls began to trot up and down the line, nervously protective. Relentlessly the shape came on. Hooves began to drum the low, deep thunder of gallop as a soundless wave of panic swept down the line. A thousand beasts began a mindless, scattering run.

Chris paused, conscious that something was happening, but puzzled by what it was. He had felt, rather than heard, the sound. A tiny vibration through the soles of his feet that had brought him to a halt abruptly, ax still raised in the air; a tremor that had risen up through his legs into his stomach, where it settled as an instinctive rumble of fear.

His head swung around, eyes searching for the source, mind racing. The lionesses had not moved, though they, too, were wakeful, alert.

He spun around to search the plain. There was nothing nearby to account for the noise.

Then his eyes swept out to the horizon. Shimmering with distance and heat, the wildebeest line was bobbing and bucking, groups of black dots shifting and re-forming, breaking away in mad, directionless dashes. Some turned back the way they had come, some went on, until a wide and ever-growing gap appeared in the line.

Through the center of the gap came a rapidly moving dark shape, trailing a cloud of dust behind it. Chris's heart turned over in his chest. Could it be? Could it possibly be? Don't shout out yet. Don't raise hopes until . . .

He cupped both hands to his forehead over his eyes.

Yes, it was. It had to be. It was moving too fast to be an animal. It was. IT WAS!

"Dad," he yelled joyously, starting to run. "There's someone coming. There's a vehicle coming this way. It's the rescue. Oh, Dad, Dad, it's all over. They've found us."

Laughing with the great joy and relief of it, he dashed back across the clearing to where his father lay. Words tumbled from him.

"Quick, quick, a shirt." He rummaged desperately in a case. "A shirt. Something to wave."

"You're sure?"

"Sure. There's someone coming. I'm sure."

"Thank God," said Mr. Harris. "Thank God. We're saved."

Chris dragged a white shirt from the case and immediately wheeled away, hurtling out through the clearing, out past the baobab, out, out onto the plain.

The vehicle was still approaching, its shape becoming more distinct now.

"Here," shouted Chris, waving the white shirt over his head. "We're here. Over here."

His heart hammered with the sheer animal pleasure of it. In a few minutes the great ordeal would be over; the terrible responsibility lifted from his slight shoulders. In a few minutes gentle hands would lift the injured, and they would be on their way, away from this horrible nightmare place, away to safety.

"Oh, quickly, quickly. We're here. We're here."

Shouting and waving, feet weightless with happiness, he ran and ran and ran. The shape became distinct. He could see that it was a Land Rover. Bouncing and bobbing and dancing over the flat green earth toward him, a sight more beautiful, more spirit-lifting than anything he had ever experienced. A Land Rover.

A dark green Land Rover.

The gap between the boy and the vehicle narrowed.

"Here. Over here." Surely they must have seen him now? He continued to run, still waving and shouting.

The Land Rover stopped.

Chris's step faltered. He slowed to a walk.

Why would they stop? he asked himself. *If they'd seen me, surely they would be coming straight on. Straight for me?*

He continued to walk toward the vehicle.

He waved again with the shirt.

"Help. Help me," he called.

The Land Rover remained motionless, its engine ticking quietly, dust settling around it. The sun was reflecting on the windshield, so Chris could not see inside.

The smile of relief died on his face now. There was something wrong. A rescue party would be around him now, shaking his hand, asking him where the others were. This motionless vehicle frightened him.

He stopped, wary and deeply dismayed, facing the vehicle.

"Hello," he called. He was shocked to find that his voice trembled. "Help me, please. I need help."

Nothing.

He wished he could see inside the cab, but the windshield was a blinding mirror, stinging his eyes.

Instinctively now he began to back away, terribly afraid of this unnaturally unresponsive vehicle with its hidden, silent occupants.

What could be wrong? Why were they not getting out? Why did they not show themselves?

He was about to turn and run back to his father, when the engine revved slightly and a metallic clunk signaled that the driver had engaged gear. Chris froze, waiting to see what would happen.

The Land Rover began to inch forward, slowly at first, then gathering momentum. There was another grinding clunk as the driver changed into second, and the vehicle accelerated rapidly.

"No," shouted Chris, "don't go. You're our only chance."

The Land Rover increased speed, heading now directly for where Chris was standing. As it approached he raised his hands in a pleading gesture, but his final, desperate "Stop . . . please stop" was drowned in engine roar as the big vehicle thundered past him.

Chapter 13

IT WAS STILL DARK WHEN HE AWOKE.

In that quiet no-man's-land between sleep and wakefulness, his mind circled like a bird seeking a place to land. He found himself transported back to an earlier occasion when he had woken under the stars.

Once, not long after his mother had died, his father had taken him camping in the Welsh mountains. Now, in those first seconds of this new day, a trick of memory spun him back there. Vividly he recalled how, on the first morning, he had woken to the soft perfume of wood smoke on the crisp air and, in the magical, silent minutes just before dawn, had thought that he could smell the sun lying just below the horizon. Many times later he had thought of that moment. Back in the city, which fogged all senses, entombed by huge, faceless buildings that shut out the clear light, amongst traffic that murdered silence and the sweet air, many times he had remembered. He had felt more alive then than at any other time. All his senses had been heightened; he could see farther, hear the tiniest rustlings of birds in the trees, smell the heavy dampness of the earth, feel all the world surrounding him on the tingling nerves of his skin. Often, drowning in classrooms, he had gazed through grimed panes onto gray, rain-swept school yards, and wished himself back there, alone in the welcoming silence of that older world.

He moved his head and looked at the fading stars. It was, he decided, the great, total silence of this place that had taken him back to that time. That and the sweet smell of the fire, which had burned all night.

He lay quiet, marveling at how aware he was, feeling his skin creep as it absorbed messages from the air. Long-unused channels were opening within him so that tiny changes of atmosphere, of sound, of unheard but felt movement, rode along his pulsing blood to trigger momentary flashes of insight in his brain. And the messages he was picking up from the unheard vibrations on the air made him uneasy.

Something was different.

The feel of the place was changed.

He sat up slowly and looked around. His father had fallen asleep, back against the rock, a branch of wood still in his hand ready to throw onto the fire.

Poor Dad. He had been determined to stay awake all night, determined that, even crippled and in pain, he would play what part he could; would watch over his son as he slept and give what protection he was capable of giving. But exhaustion and worry had defeated him. In the red fire-glow, shadows lined his face deeply, and profound black holes engulfed his eyes. He looked very old, Chris thought. Even in sleep the corners of his mouth sagged in pain.

Dimly, out on the plain, the mushroom shapes of the acacia trees began to emerge black and mysterious against a faintly lightening sky.

Almost dawn. Soon he would have to go.

He shivered, partly from the morning chill, partly from a sudden rush of fear, which made his stomach lurch. He took a deep, gasping breath, caught the fear, and held it down. There was no place for fear now. Fear would blur judgment. Every move, every decision now, was a fine weight on a balance. The balance of life and death. Every calculation must be cool and rational. One brief moment of panic could mean the end of them all.

The fear subsided. The trick was not to think too much. Get up, do the things that have to be done, and go. Don't let the thought of what might happen gain a foothold. Do as the animals do; watch everything, hear everything, let the world tell you through the ends of your nerves what you must do; and then do it. Melt into this place. Feel it. And beat it at its own game.

He got to his feet and stood very still and very silent. His unease remained. Something intangible, some invisible, inaudible warning was tapping at the door of his mind. He closed his eyes, the better to see what lay outside, beyond his vision. As yet he could not say what was there, could not decode the vibrating message. Like a fisherman casting a fly he tried to throw his mind out onto the plain, searching, searching for the young lion. Perhaps he had moved back closer; perhaps in the dark hours he had healed his dignity and had returned.

The plain remained dark, silent, and empty to Chris's searching mind. Wherever the animal was, he was not close. Chris was sure of that. Malevolence surrounded the beast, lay on the air as heavy and as tangible as a gathering thunderstorm. If he was close Chris would surely know it.

He shook his head. The message on the air was not this. The unease remained. He moved it temporarily to the back of his mind.

Picking up the plastic water bottle, he crossed the gradually lightening clearing to where the pilot lay. The man had moved slightly so that his head lay to one side and tilted backward, his mouth open. The ghostly predawn light tinged his flesh gray. The deep shadows of his eyes and the black gaping mouth turned the head into a grinning skull, an effigy of death that brought Chris's heart into his throat. But it was only a trick of the light, for the man still breathed, though shallowly and with quick, gasping gulps.

Gently Chris raised the man's head and placed it back onto the pillow of clothes. He dribbled a little water onto a piece of torn sheet and held it to the dry, cracked lips, squeezing a few drops of water into his mouth. He dare not give him too much in case he choked. The man groaned faintly at the touch of the water, and his tongue moved against his lips. Chris placed his hand on the man's forehead. His skin was cold and damp, the clamminess of deep shock pervading him. His time was running out rapidly now.

"Just a little longer," whispered Chris, as he carefully laid the wet rag against the pilot's lips. "Just hang on a little longer."

He stood and looked down at the injured man for a moment, wondering about him. Was there someone at home waiting, anxious and fearful for him? Someone now perhaps wondering if they would ever see their husband or their dad again?

He sighed and turned away. There was nothing more he could do for this poor, broken body; nothing but what he was doing. He hoped against hope that he would be in time to save him.

The light was increasing rapidly now, the heavy grayness turning to silver on the horizon. Soon the first crescent of sun would creep up on the rim of the plain and he would go. In the dying minutes of yesterday he had used the westerly setting sun to point his arrow compass northwest. Now he needed only to wait for daylight so he could find some distant, easily identifiable landmark to aim for.

He moved quietly back to the bivouac and made his final preparations. Taking one of his shirts from a case, he swung it onto his head so that the back of the shirt hung down over his neck and shoulders like a cape. He crossed the arms of the shirt over his forehead and knotted them at the back of his head. Yesterday he had been able to hide from the noonday sun. Today, unless he took precautions, it might just kill him. He took off his shoes and from his case pulled his ancient, well-loved, battered training shoes. Three lives depended on his feet; they must be given no chance to fail him. The worn contours of the shoes slipped into place like another skin. He laced them carefully but tightly. The all-important water bottle, the fruit, and a small packet of crackers he placed in an old canvas holdall that he would be able to don like a knapsack. This he laid on the ground at the side of the machete.

He was ready. All he needed now was the light.

The silver of the horizon was now fanned by long streaks of gold shooting up from the edge of the world. The great plain was gradually taking form under his eyes, the ground lightening by the minute. The trees melted from black to soft brown, their flat tops catching the dancing light between their branches so that they shimmered silver, as though they swarmed with fireflies.

He breathed deeply of the sweet morning air. Once more he was struck by the languid vastness, the incomprehensible, primeval indifference of this great, empty land. Africa, he was beginning to feel, was a huge hibernating animal, not a land at all. An animal suspended, entranced by time and silence; an animal overtaken by torpor, breathing out its days in quiet, sweet breaths whilst, on its back, countless minute dramas arose and vanished in the blink of an eye. But now he was no longer afraid, no longer dismayed. He had found, in the extremity of the circumstances that had hurled them all to the very edges of survival, that there was, deep inside of him, a strength, never suspected because never before needed, which he could count on. And that, he decided, gave him some rights. Chris Harris—tiny speck of life amongst a teeming multitude of lives—had, in these few, short hours of cataclysmic upheaval, earned his place on this planet. Chris Harris had, in short, earned the right to live.

He took a last look at his dad and, for a few seconds only, pondered whether to wake him to say their good-byes. He decided against it. The night fading gradually to day had given him strength. Nothing must disturb his confidence now. Good-byes were too dangerous. Unnecessary, too, he decided. They both knew the risks. Both knew that this had to be done.

"So, let's do it," Chris said to himself, and he bent to pick up the holdall and machete.

The moment had come.

Taking a deep breath, he slipped his arms into the handles of the holdall and swung it up onto his back. He took a brief look around the clearing. He etched it deep into his mind. This place, he thought, this strange, alien place would live in minute, photographic detail in his mind for all of his days. This place of pain and terror looked less fearsome now as confidence painted new colors into it with the quick brush strokes of his eyes. "Familiarity breeds confidence," he said to himself and smiled.

And yet . . . the unease he had felt earlier remained. It gnawed at him. Something was different. Something hung on the air, calling to him. The feel of the place was still wrong.

For the last time he tried closing his eyes and feeling the place with his mind.

He scanned, like a camera, around the perimeter of the clearing. There was only silence and the soft threat of building heat.

He flicked inward to the wreckage. Nothing.

Out to the baobab. Nothing.

Back in. Nothing.

Up to the face of the kopje.

He paused.

That was it. The change was there—on the kopje.

He explored it carefully now, eyes flicking from rock to rock, mind stretching out to read what was written there. Yellowed by the soft rising sunlight it stood silent, at peace.

And he knew.

The pride was gone.

In the days to come he would ask himself many times how he had known this thing. He would never answer the question.

Yet know he did—and at the moment of knowing a great surging sadness filled him.

For he also knew another thing.

That the old, tired, injured beast whose mind had so briefly touched his in that split second of understanding, of insight, remained. Alone.

He stood, staring long at the kopje face. He had the overwhelming feeling that his fate was somehow inexplicably bound up with that of this strange, wild creature. That time, circumstance, fate, if you like, had brought them together.

He called to the animal.

I know, he called with his mind. *I know what's happened—what's happening. Don't give up. I'm not giving up. I'm going to live. You live, too.*

He stared hard at the kopje, trying to drive his mind-message deep into the rocks.

Live, he called. *Live*.

Then he turned, fixed his eye on a low, blue hill to the northwest and walked quietly but determinedly out of the clearing. A small figure walking off into the vastness of Serengeti.

And as he walked away, he fancied he heard, so faint that he could not be sure he really heard anything, a long, low animal cry of pain.

On the other side of the kopje a solitary figure dropped silently down onto the plain.

The night chill had stiffened his bones and he groaned softly as he moved.

The wound in his flank hurt. He turned his great head to lick at the pain. That done, his head swung back again and his eyes scanned the shining distances.

He stood—waiting now.

A force was stirring, deep within him. He knew, as his old mind took stock of the new day, that things were ending for him. The battle with the young lion had taken its toll, and in his heart was the knowledge that he would not survive another.

There was a lonely silence hanging over the kopje. The lionesses and cubs had gone during the night, and instinct told him that they were not merely out hunting. They had deserted him. Even now they were out on the plain, making up to the young outsider.

He snarled softly to himself.

There was, of course, no sadness, no regret.

But there was knowledge, knowledge that the circle of his life was almost closed. The circle that had encompassed his growth; the days of the hunt and the kill; the days when he had roamed wide on the plains establishing his own territory after he had been driven out of his birth pride; the days of siring and protecting; the proud, proud days of his pride. All were over now.

And he was to be driven out again. Soon the lionesses and cubs would return. They would not return alone. His adversary would be with them.

And they would be returning to take possession of the kopje.

There was now, he knew, no place for him here.

The moment had come when the last tiny gap in the circle needed to be closed.

He would leave, quietly. He had earned the right to bring his days to a peaceful end. To close the circle with equanimity. To lie down in calm and safety and let the struggle fade.

There was a deep longing in him. A longing to return. Just where to return he was not sure, but his instincts were beginning to recall the place. The place before this one, the place before the years of nomadic searching, the place of his youth and growing.

The place of his birth. There he would return to die.

And so, as the first warm light of the day began to lift the ghost-white mists of Serengeti, he waited. A long, long wait until instinct, long-dead memory, awakened and gave him direction.

Homing instinct. The way home.

Eventually the great weary head turned slightly. The questing, amber eyes became still and settled on a low, blue hill, shimmered by distance.

And he began to walk, slowly but determinedly, away from the kopje. An old, faded, faltering figure walking off into the vastness of Serengeti.

And as he walked away, he gave a faint, long, low cry, half anger, half pain.

No sadness, no regret—animals do not feel these things.

Just the instinctive cry of an old animal in pain.

Chapter 14

IT WAS BARELY EIGHT O'CLOCK, YET ALREADY THE SUN was pouring heat down on them and the metal of the Land Rover was too hot to touch. The American had perched himself on the spare wheel on the hood, where he sat disconsolately viewing the surrounding emptiness, eyes screwed up against the glare. Finally he nodded to himself and gave his verdict.

"Jeez," he said, and fell silent again.

They were just north of Naabi Hill, stopped on the red dust road that heads north through Seronera and Lobo to the Kenyan border. Bennie was stamping irritably on a foot pump to inflate a mournful-looking rear tire, grumbling softly but vehemently to himself in Swahili.

"What's he goddamn muttering about?"

"He's exploring the possibility of the *fundi* who

repaired our punctures in Arusha being the offspring of a union not sanctified by holy matrimony," replied Mike, who was standing high up on the roof rack scanning the surrounding plains through his binoculars.

"Hmm. That applies to a lot of people I know," said Hyram. "Why him in particular?"

"Unless you watch their every move they steal your good inner tubes and replace them with worn-out, perished junk with about a hundred patches in already. They should send budding magicians to this country. What Tanzanians don't know about sleight of hand isn't worth knowing. They can pick your pockets without coming within twenty feet of you."

Bennie quietly swore his agreement and continued stamping irascibly.

"Anyway, more to the point," continued the tourist, "can you see anything?"

"Nothing," replied Mike. "Absolutely nothing."

"Wonderful." Hyram spat disgustedly into the red dust. "I thought you Great White Hunters were supposed to be able to track anything. You follow spoor and droppings and stuff, and notice little things that ordinary people like me don't, like bent grass and broken twigs. I know that—I seen John Wayne do it. And here we are—out there there's a ton and a half of goddamn Land Rover crashing about the place, leaving a track like a Sherman tank, and we've lost it."

Turning slowly, Mike continued his three-hundred-and-sixty-degree search.

"I've got news for you," he retorted. "This isn't the films—it's real life. And I'm not Davy Crockett."

"That's obvious," replied Hyram, without malice.

He turned his attention to the heavily perspiring Bennie.

"And what about you? Do you know where they are? Ain't you Africans supposed to know about this stuff? In tune with the land, super-hearing, sixth sense, dark forces lost to the white man and all that?"

"Not me, bwana." Bennie grinned. He was beginning to like this gruff, down-to-earth man with his strange direct talking. "I'm a city boy. I don't know anything except driving Land Rovers. I just do what I'm told."

"Most of the time," added a voice from the roof rack.

"Most of the time," agreed Bennie.

There was a pause—the silence of the plains broken only by the squeak and wheeze of the foot pump.

The American swiped absently at a mosquito on his leg, then began to sing softly:

"Here we sit like birds in the wilderness,
Birds in the wilderness, birds in the wilderness."

"Oh, for goodness' sake," snapped Mike, jumping down from the roof rack. "I told you last night it was no good. These people are professionals—they spend their lives being chased by police, customs, anti-poaching squads, villagers, everybody. Their business, and their lives, depend on being able to escape, to vanish into thin air. If they can give everybody else the slip, what chance do we stand?"

"Yeah, yeah—I know. It just seems, well—so near, so far, if you know what I mean. It's disappointing. What they did back there—that's the worst thing I ever seen. Don't get me wrong—I ain't led no sheltered life. I seen animals killed before. I seen men killed in Korea. And I ain't no animal rights nut, nor nothing like that. But somehow—I can't explain it too well—somehow, there's fair and there's not fair. That back there was not fair. Somehow it outrages me."

"You don't have to explain," said Mike, returning his binoculars into their case. "I know the feeling."

"I know you know," continued Hyram. "And I know something else. When you shot at them—they weren't no warning shots, they weren't no low shots to injure. You would have killed them if you could. You would have taken them out one by one and enjoyed every second of it."

"Every second." Mike nodded, stony-faced, as he remembered his disgust, his blind anger and hatred of the senseless, mindless slaughter of yesterday.

He looked inquiringly now at the American. The shared experience of yesterday, the shared horror and revulsion, had revealed to them both more about each other than many people learn about others in a lifetime. Watching the hunched shoulders, white face, and tear-filled eyes of the bluff, loud-mouthed tourist yesterday, as they stood in that awful, charnel-house scene, had given Mike a deep sympathy for this man. He was not at all what his surface portrayed, and the man underneath the façade commanded respect and attention.

"You're leading up to something, aren't you?" he asked. "I'm getting to recognize signs about you. You've got something else you want to say, haven't you?"

"Yep," replied Hyram. "I've got something else to say. But I ain't going to say it because you'll bang me in the mouth if I do."

Mike looked at him, wondering whether he was serious. He decided he was.

"Say it anyway, and I'll try and restrain myself."

The American paused a little, then nodded.

"OK, Mr. Taylor. Here it comes. Try this for size."

He eased himself out of the spare wheel, sat on the front of the hood, and looked steadily at Mike.

"You got a weakness. I seen it before, in the army. It's a dangerous weakness, and you know you've got it, and it's the reason we've lost those guys." He paused a second to gauge the effect he was having.

"Go on," said Mike. His lips felt a little tight as he said it, and he could feel color beginning to rise to his cheeks. "Though I think I know what you're going to say, and I may well 'bang you in the mouth,' as you so delicately put it."

"There you go again. See, that proves it. That's what I was going to tell you. Anger. That's your weakness. Any second now you're going to start banging about like a lunatic in a padded cell, slamming things in and out of the Land Rover, biting the heads off us all, and sending this driver of yours off in five different directions at once. Just like you did yesterday."

He climbed down off the Land Rover and stood facing Mike.

"So, if that's the way you want to do things, let's get on with it. Let's get in the goddamn Land Rover, point it to goddamn nowhere, and goddamn drive there at a hundred goddamn miles a goddamn hour. Then when we've got to nowhere we can sit there and wonder where the hell we are and why we ain't found them goddamn poachers. Just like we did yesterday. And just like we're doing now."

The two men stood facing each other, silent now. Bennie had frozen, mouth hanging open, one leg still poised over the pump. Awaiting the inevitable violent explosion—which, miraculously, never came. There was a long, long pause—during which Mike stood statuelike, fists clenched, knuckles white. Slowly the flush and the tightness began to drain from his face. Then he turned and walked a few feet away, keeping his back to the American.

"Phew," said Bennie, and he shook his head.

"Phew," said Mike Taylor at last. "Anything else?"

"No, that'll do for now," said the American simply.

"Right." Mike turned and, amazingly, was smiling. The forthrightness of the man had defeated his anger. He was right, of course—and Mike knew it only too well. A fault that had dogged him all his life—a fault he had tried again and again to control and had almost always failed. In his fifty years, this flaw, this black-eyed rage at cruelty and senseless killing, had led him into more dangers, and more importantly, more failures, than he would care to admit even to himself.

And there was a further component to this equation. Anger leads to failure. Failure leads to guilt. Guilt leads to more anger. At some stage the circle, truly a vicious circle, has to be broken and rational thought allowed in. This almost-stranger had told him something that friends, if he had had any left, would never have dared to tell him to his face. This man had put his finger on the nerve and broken the circle.

"OK," said Mike. "I accept the criticism. Presumably all this is leading up to something. The lecture wasn't for the good of my psychological health. Would you like to get to the point?"

"Yep. The point is this. There's fair and there's unfair. I don't like unfair. I don't like what I saw, and every time I think about it, it turns my stomach.

137

And you were about to suggest that we give up the chase and go back to the goddamn hotel and let those guys get away."

"We've lost the trail," shouted Mike in exasperation. "For goodness' sake, we've lost the flaming trail. What do you want me to do—stand and shout 'Come back, you're under arrest' and hope they do?"

"We can sit down and talk about possibilities, that's what. I'm not a fool. I know we don't stand much chance of ever finding them, but I tell you I'll sure sleep much better if we make one last try to find their trail again. And I'd have felt a whole lot better if once, just once, you'd asked me what I thought or what I wanted to do, instead of just roaring about the goddamn countryside looking as if you were going to kick the windshield to death."

Mike was forced to laugh. The picture was too accurate, too horribly familiar, for him to take offense.

"Right," he said after a pause, and he held out his hand to the American. They shook. "You're absolutely right. I behaved like a spoiled child. I apologize."

"Don't bother apologizing. Just tell me we can have one last try before we head back."

"OK," Mike agreed, "but honestly, the chances are a million to one. They could be anywhere."

"These people. They're not Tanzanians, eh?"

"No—Somalis. That doesn't help us. They won't be heading back there until they've sold the ivory."

"Where will they do that?"

"Depends how desperate they are. If they're really desperate they can sell it in Tanzania or Uganda, but the prices aren't so good. The big ivory merchants are in Nairobi. And they'll pay in U.S. dollars—that's what these people really want. Half the African countries' currencies are worthless—U.S. dollars make you a wealthy man, you can spend them anywhere. Those tusks they're carrying are worth their weight in transistor radios, watches, jeans, and all the other rubbish we've taught the African to need."

"So, they're heading for Kenya. Presumably they can't just arrive at the border post with six feet of tusk sticking out the back of the vehicle and two guys bleeding all over the road from bullet holes."

"They won't go near any border posts. They'll have any number of places they can cross without being seen. It's anybody's guess which they'll choose."

"Right. Let's think for a moment. Put yourself in the driver's position. He's on the run with two injured men. He'll expect that we've informed the authorities and that people on both sides of the border will be looking for them. What would you do in his position?"

Mike thought for a moment.

"I wouldn't be in a hurry about crossing. I'd want to get help for the injured men—that would be better done in Tanzania; bullet holes would cause more questions in Kenya than they do here. And I'd want a few days for things to cool down before attempting the border anyway, in case patrols were out. Bennie, bring the map, will you?"

"Yes, boss." Bennie reached in through the Land Rover window and emerged with a dog-eared sheet that he opened on the hood.

"Here's Seronera." Mike placed his finger on the map. "Yesterday we headed out on this track that runs below Nyabogati. That's a Masai village of about a hundred people or so. We turned south before the Wasso road."

He continued tracing his finger down the map.

"It would be about here we came on the wildebeest migration, so I reckon we met the poachers just about here." He placed his finger on the *t* of "Serengeti."

"Right." Hyram took up the thread. "Then you left them your little calling card, but they didn't want to stay to your party and shot off to the west—am I right?"

"Yes, you're right. But they wouldn't keep going west—they'd double back."

"Why do you say that?"

"They wouldn't want to cross the main Ngorongoro–Seronera road. That's a well-used road—they'd steer clear of that for fear of being spotted. My guess is that once they'd got well clear of us they'd turn and head north. Look, there's nothing between these two roads—not a village, not a settlement of any kind, except Nyabogati—between here and the Kenyan border."

He started to fold the map. "So, that's it—that's my guess. They're still in here somewhere—close to Nyabogati. That's quite a large village by Serengeti standards, and there'll be a village healer there where they can buy some magic potion or other for the wounds. They'll hole up somewhere near there, and then, in a few days, sneak across the border at night and drive into Nairobi under cover of darkness."

"Unless we stop them," said Hyram, darkly.

"Unless we stop them," agreed Mike.

"Look," he added, "I know how you feel, and I understand completely why you want to do something about them. But it's one thing looking at a map and talking—it's quite another finding them. All I'm prepared to do is this. We'll head for Nyabogati. We'll go slowly and we'll look carefully. But once we get to Nyabogati, that's it. If we haven't found them by then, we pack it in and go straight back to Seronera. Agreed?"

"Who's paying for this goddamn safari?" asked the American.

Mike shrugged resignedly. "OK, then. If you put it that way. What do you suggest?"

"I suggest we head for this Nya place you're talking about. I suggest we go slowly and keep our eyes open. And I suggest that if we don't find anything today, we pack it in and go straight back to Seronera."

Mike gave a helpless sigh and shook his head.

"Marvelous," he said. "That sounds to me a wonderful plan. I wish I'd thought of it."

"So, there you are. All we needed was a bit of brains and a bit of perseverence. If you're all done standing around wasting time and fiddling about with tires, perhaps we could get along. Why don't we sit this man of yours up on the roof rack. He'll stand more chance of seeing any wheel tracks from up there."

"Bennie," ordered Mike. "Upstairs."

"Aw, bwana, please no. Not on the roof."

"Bennie, I've got quite enough on my plate arguing with this unreasonable, thoroughly pigheaded, rude man here. Will you please just humor him and do as you are told." He spoke through clenched teeth.

Hyram grinned happily. "There's a twenty-dollar bill in my wallet got your name on it if you spot anything," he added by way of encouragement.

"Twenty dollars!" exclaimed Bennie. "Twenty American dollars." He was already climbing onto the roof rack as he was speaking. "Let's go, boss. What are we waiting for?"

"Indeed," said Mike with the air of a defeated man. "What are we waiting for?"

And he climbed into the driving seat and started the engine.

The American stood for a moment staring hard at the northern horizon.

"OK, you guys," he said to the hills in the distance, "start praying. We're coming for you."

Mike let in the clutch and the Land Rover began to inch quietly forward.

"You coming? Or are you going to stand there talking to the grass?" he called.

Hyram pulled open the passenger door and climbed aboard as the vehicle continued to move. As he slammed the door, Mike accelerated down the road, then swung the Land Rover off the red dust onto the grass.

"Due north," he said. "Slow, but sure."

"Yep."

"Twenty dollars," Mike mused. "If Bennie doesn't find them for twenty dollars, then they're not here."

"By the way," he added after a pause, "do you know how to shoot?"

"Jeez," said the American. "He asks me if I know how to shoot." He spat disgustedly out of the window. "I'm a New Yorker. In New York you're born knowing how to shoot. Just find those guys, will you—then we'll talk about who can shoot."

"You're the boss," said Mike. And they settled to the laborious business of cross-country driving, the sweet, whining song of the Land Rover rising and falling in front of them.

Chapter 15

THERE IS A FEELING THAT PLAGUES ALL SOLITARY TRAV-
elers, and it was nagging at Chris as he walked.

The feeling that he was not alone.

Of course the traveler on Serengeti is far from
alone. Every step Chris took was followed by appraising eyes. He didn't see most of them—most
were hidden by trees, or long grass, or vast
distance—but they all saw him. Some were wildly
fearful, their owners poised for flight should his direction change. Others were narrowed, boring a
shaft of malice at him through the air.

But most quickly became indifferent. In the midst
of multitudes he was of concern to none. In the midst
of multitudes he was left alone.

Chris soon learned this lesson. Fearful at first, he
had approached the great herds of antelope, gazelle,
and wildebeest cautiously, only to find a pattern re-

peated again and again. A pattern of raised, attentive heads, nostrils widened to seek his intention, then a quick scattering and reassembling out of danger. And the way, like the Red Sea, parted for him to pass through.

But there was something else. The odd shadow flitting just beyond his field of vision; the presence behind his back that raised the hair on his neck but, as his anxious head swung around, was not there; the movement of grass that was not the wind; the cry he almost heard in the distance.

So, although his confidence grew as the miles accumulated under his feet, it was tempered with constant, instinctive vigilance. Tiny prickles of fear would jolt him and deflect his path from certain trees, certain holes in the ground, certain hillocks. Why, he did not know, but his senses would make him pause, listen, differentiate between safety and danger, and make his movement accordingly.

The walking was easy. In happier, less urgent circumstances, it would have been a pleasure. Aeons past, when the world was fire, the titanic explosions of Ngorongoro, Oldonyo Lengai, and Meru had laid a thick bed of volcanic dust and ash upon this plain. Time had turfed it into a fertile, sprung carpet. Walking upon it was like walking on a fine lawn. Chris felt light of body and had fallen into an easy, rolling rhythm.

And gradually the low, blue hill crept closer to him. Once there he would be able to look back to the kopje, line up his bearing with another distinctive landmark, and proceed. Sooner or later he would strike the road, and safety.

From the position of the sun he guessed it was about eleven o'clock. The heat was building now, and the gash on his head was beginning to throb a little. Not enough to slow him, but enough to be troublesome. The shirt he had tied for protection around his head was rubbing the open wound. He decided to rest for a few minutes and headed for a lone baobab, which stood like a huge tattered beggarman, arms limply imploring from a tangle of rags. The ancient tree, with its massive central bulk, threw a cool cave of shade onto the ground, where he could escape briefly from the glare. He plunged thankfully into it, slipped the bag from his shoulders, and sat down. He removed the shirt from his head and laid it across his knees, took his precious water bottle from the bag and, careful not to waste any of the water, wetted the shirt. He folded the shirt carefully again and retied it round his head. The coolness of it brought instant relief to the throbbing wound, and he sighed gratefully and leaned back against the tree trunk to rest.

He sat, nibbling a cracker and enjoying the freedom from motion and vigilance. The tree and the shade somehow exuded safety, however temporary, however illusory.

Like an animal finding a lair, thought Chris.

Cocooned by shade and silence, he felt strangely

protected by this tree. He moved his head and looked upward at the massive trunk rearing above him. The bark hung like long ragged strips of skin flayed from the body. Great, deeply gouged wounds, riven by elephant tusks, exposed the inner flesh, white and fibrous. A soft, fruitlike smell surrounded the tree, like an unharvested orchard in autumn, heavily over-ripe, beginning to ferment. Chris found the smell curiously soporific, and he closed his eyes briefly, luxuriating in the shaded, perfumed silence.

His eyes drooped.

A short sleep couldn't hurt.

He'd been walking, he guessed, for more than four hours.

Another hour should see him at the hill.

Soon it would be the hottest part of the day, when he shouldn't walk anyway.

Just a short sleep.

There's no danger here.

Everything sleeps as the day moves toward noon.

His head began to droop to his chest.

His eyes closed.

In the final seconds before sleep overcame him he thought he heard, just for a moment or two, a low humming sound in the distance.

But it faded, then stopped.

He slept.

The lion was limping heavily now. The smell of blood from the deep wound in his flank had brought the tsetse flies. They covered the gash, obscene, seething like maggots, a black boiling tumor biting into him. They ignored his wafting tail. Periodically he would slump to the ground and savagely lick and snap them away. But the relief was short-lived. As soon as he arose and resumed his dogged but pained pilgrimage, they swarmed back, plunging into him, drilling his flesh, angering and wearying.

And his weariness was almost total now. His head hung below his shoulders as he walked. He looked defeated. Even the timid gazelles sensed that there was nothing to fear from him, and instead of scattering like flocks of startled birds at his approach, they merely walked quietly aside and continued grazing as he passed. The king no longer looked a king. His subjects no longer bowed to him.

He was oblivious to them anyway. Only one thought filled his mind now, a relentlessly persistent voice calling him. From somewhere out in the shimmering mist of distance it pulsed, a steady beat, a siren heartbeat calling him home. Beating around him and within him, it was taking over his functions. The beat *was* his heartbeat. The beat drove his every step. Like a dying patient on a life support machine, he felt the distant pulse become his pulse, pulling him step by weary step. A slow, halting progress toward the long, low hill where he could lie, at last in peace, to bring his life, in quiet dignity, to its close.

He needed to rest again. The flies and the building

heat of midmorning were tormenting his wound. He smelled water and turned off his arrow-straight path, dropping down into a small depression where a cool, clear pool of water lay. A lone zebra, startled at his approach, scurried away, then turned and watched as the old figure drank gratefully. Shadows flitted momentarily across the surface of the water as two vultures glided silently across the sky above him, slapped their wings, and landed heavily in a thorn tree. He growled a warning, but both they and he knew it was a hollow threat. Drawn by the certainty of death, they would remain with him now, the sole, implacable witnesses to his final hours. Watchers and waiters of terrible, voracious patience.

He walked into the shallow water and eased his hurt flank down into the coolness of it. The flies rose from the wound and buzzed angrily around him for a while. He snapped halfheartedly at them until eventually they abandoned him and dispersed, droning heavy with his blood, to seek prey elsewhere.

The cool water brought instant relief from the hurt. He laid his big, tired head down at the pool edge and closed his eyes. There was no danger for him here. As the day pads heavily toward noon, all things sleep.

He began to drift off.

In the final seconds before sleep overcame him, his ears twitched at a low humming sound in the distance.

But it gradually faded, then stopped.

He slept.

Chris's sleep was so deep that the soft purr of the Land Rover as it crept up to the tree did not wake him. So deep that the metallic click of the door catch went unheard, as did the hurried, urgent whisperings. His sleep was broken by a sharp pain in his leg from a heavy kick.

"So, *mzungu*," barked a harsh voice, "we find you again."

Startled and disoriented for a second, Chris cried out as he awoke; an instinctive, almost animal yelp of fear. In his sleep he had rolled down and onto his side. He opened his eyes and saw nothing.

"Sit up, white boy," snarled the voice, heavy with menace, from behind him.

Sharp terror shot through him. He yelped again as something hard poked him in the back, and he rolled desperately away. As he rolled over he looked up, trembling now with shock. Momentarily his mind went numb as he took in what he saw.

Towering over him was a huge black man, wearing only khaki shorts; in his hands the gun that had just jabbed Chris in the back. Behind him, just beyond the tree, the dark green Land Rover, which had so mysteriously and callously driven past yesterday.

The man was smiling. Not a welcoming smile, a calculating, sneering smile.

"Where you keep springing from, white boy? Eh?"
Chris remained silent, numbed with shock.

"So, the white boy cannot speak." He grinned, widely and contemptuously, revealing blackened teeth filed to sharp points. The savage strangeness of his mouth heightened Chris's fear, so alien did it seem.

"Sit there, white boy. Don't move. Don't make a sound."

He called out something in another language, and the passenger door of the Land Rover clicked open. Another man revealed himself, slumped heavily in the seat, around his leg a heavily bloodstained bandage. He eased himself painfully around and looked hard at the boy. His face was less baleful, less coldly mocking, and his voice, when it came, less harsh than his companion's.

"What are you doing here, boy? Where do you think you are going?"

"Please," said Chris, his voice made high and wavery by his fear, "please, we had an accident. Our plane crashed, back there near some rocks." He pointed back toward the kopje. "Two men are injured, my father and the pilot. I have to find help. Please help me. Please—just take me to where I can get help . . . We could pay you," he added as an afterthought.

He stopped and looked at their faces, but could read nothing in them. The savage grin still remained on the face of the man closest to him, who said after a short pause, "Oh yes, boy, I think you will pay us." He chuckled grimly in his throat.

"Stay there," he snarled again and, turning his back on Chris, loped back to the Land Rover. Chris watched warily as the two men talked quietly to each other. He tried to stop himself trembling but could not. Briefly he thought of running—but what was the point? The Land Rover would easily catch him. And where would he run to anyway?

He was at their mercy—and these men looked as though they would have little of that commodity. The elephant tusks in the back of the vehicle and the bloodstained bandages told him that these men were dangerous. But, even men like this, he thought, could not refuse to help a young boy, desperate and alone, fighting for his life and the lives of others. They couldn't refuse. Could they?

The men were talking so quietly that he could not hear what they said. They probably weren't using English anyway, he guessed. But there was something about the urgency and earnestness of the way they spoke that gave Chris a deep unease.

The injured man spoke, finally, to him.

"All right, boy. Come. We will take you with us. We will take you to help."

Though the voice was quiet and held no threat, the relief that should have flooded through Chris's mind did not come. The words were right—exactly what he had hoped to hear.

152

The words were right. But the message was wrong. The eyes held the truth—the eyes remained cold. No compassion, no sympathy, matched the words.

The words were a lie. Take him they would. But to help themselves, not him.

Suddenly it was clear. They would use him. These men, so obviously criminal, needed him to escape. He was their passport. They would pass wherever they wished, unharmed and unhindered, because they held a small white boy to bargain their freedom with.

That was the truth.

Too frightened for rational thought, Chris was lanced by this truth. This would be the end of all his chances. The end of him, and the end of the men who depended upon him. He saw clearly that if he were to go with these men, he would never be released alive.

No matter now that there was nowhere to run to. His brain said run away. In an instant he was on his feet. Before even the wave of surprise had formed on the faces of the two men, he was away and running, blind panic coursing adrenaline through him. On the wind, racing past his ears, he heard a shouted command. He glanced back over his shoulder and saw the man with the gun take a step forward and raise it to his shoulder.

"Stop," he cried. "Stop or I'll shoot."

Chris began to weave, still racing at top speed, his heart pounding. Three steps to the right, three to the left. He heard the sharp crack of a shot, then, a microsecond later, a high whistle of air as the bullet whooshed past him. He was almost beyond fear now. His mind had blocked everything but the urgent command to his body to hurl itself away. He weaved constantly, awaiting the second shot, all the while running as he had never run before, his feet pounding the soft earth, his arms pumping hard to give himself all the speed his frame was capable of.

The second shot did not come.

Quickly he glanced over his shoulder again, a split-second glance only. The man had left the Land Rover and was in pursuit of him on foot.

His brain began to work again. A stroke of luck, this. If the man had had the wit to jump in the Land Rover straight away, all would have been lost. They would have caught him in minutes. But now there was a chance, small chance though it was. Chris was young and very fast. The man would have to be very fit indeed to catch him. And by the time he realized that he couldn't and returned to get the Land Rover to chase him, Chris would have put a good distance between them. Perhaps then he would be able to hide until they gave up. There was already several hundred yards between them. He was heading still for the hill that had been his landmark all morning. If he could make it over that, he might be able to find a hiding place on the other side. From the hill he might even be able to see the road he was seeking.

Only one thing remained.

The gun.

He had not had time, in his brief glance, to take in whether the man still had the gun. Quickly he glanced back again, narrowing his eyes against the sun's glare, to get his answer.

That was his undoing. In those brief seconds when his eyes left the ground in front of him, his foot plunged into a hole in the turf, twisting his ankle so ferociously that it flung him completely off balance. He was hurled heavily to the ground, rolling over and over. He came to a stop, gasping for air, which the fall had slammed out of him. Instantly he was on his feet again, but the first step he took shot a searing bolt of pain up through his leg and into his body. He screamed with the pain of it—but still he tried again.

It was no good. The ankle was so badly twisted that the pain was insupportable.

Still driven, he limped another few steps before slumping to his knees.

It was the end, he knew.

He had tried and failed.

In a few moments the man would be upon him, and Chris would be at the mercy of his whim.

Those depending on Chris would die.

Perhaps he would die.

But now there was nothing left that he could do.

Sobbing with the pain, the fear, and the sorrow, he turned and sat, holding his injured leg, as the man loped toward him with long easy strides.

Ironically Chris saw that he did not have the gun in his hands anyway. He had dropped it to give chase. The fatal glance had not been necessary. If only he had just concentrated on running and kept his eyes to the front.

It was all too much.

Perhaps he had been presumptuous anyway. How could he ever have thought that there was a chance in any of this?

How could he ever have thought that a young boy could take on Africa and win?

So now it was the end. There were no more decisions to make, no more responsibilities to shoulder, no more battles to fight.

Defeated, he watched the man approach.

He had slowed now to a walk, confident of his prey, the contemptuous grin returning to his face.

He was only two hundred yards away now.

Then a hundred.

Then fifty.

Again Chris began to tremble as the figure came closer and closer.

Would the man hurt him?

He couldn't take any more hurt.

He wished that he could die. The nightmare had become too much for his young mind to stand. Death was preferable to what could happen to him at the hands of these vicious, desperate men.

The man had stopped about twenty yards from where Chris sat fearfully awaiting him. Hands on hips, legs apart, mocking. The cruel face grinned savagely at him.

"So, white boy," he began, shaking his head in admonition. "So, now you come with us."

His hands dropped from his hips and he started to walk toward Chris.

"On your feet, white boy."

Chris did not, could not, move.

The man's lips curled back over his filed teeth. His grin had gone and taking its place was a sneer of such savagery, such viciousness, that a huge wave of fear rose up from Chris's stomach.

The man's right hand went to his back pocket. When it reappeared it held a small but wickedly pointed knife.

He spoke again.

"I said, on your—"

He did not finish.

He stopped.

The lion snarled even before his eyes flicked open. He rolled instinctively onto his feet and stood listening. Where that sound was, man was. Where that sound was, danger and death were not far behind.

The cool water had eased his pain and his weariness. He was refreshed, alert. He could not see beyond the sides of the depression, but his ears searched.

Another sound came. He had been right. It was man. A man voice. He snarled again, a low hatred.

157

These creatures above all, he feared. Especially now when he knew that he was no longer fleet. Even in his prime he had known better than to face man. Only a cornered or injured animal will face man.

But he was both injured and cornered.

Cornered by age.

He felt the vibrations of running feet in the ground beneath him. A lifetime of listening and feeling confirmed that they were human feet, running toward him.

Too old and stubborn to run, he curled his lips back over his teeth in a silent challenge, and he moved forward, away from the water, and started up the side of the rise.

Another human cry—a cry this time of pain and fear.

He hesitated. The running stopped.

He waited motionless, silent, hardly breathing.

Was the danger over?

Then another deeper voice, this one threatening. The man was waiting for him. Just over the crest the man was there.

He pulled his head up high. His age and weariness and injury forgotten as the battle instinct flooded through his blood, he began to move, gathering speed as he climbed, until he came over the top of the rise like a gold lightning flash.

He probably didn't even see the boy slumped on the ground, holding his leg.

But he saw the man.

And his huge jaws began to open as he bounded toward him.

The man was frozen in midstep, like a puppet suspended on strings. His eyes, Chris saw, had flicked upward to a point somewhere behind Chris's head. The vicious snarling face was transformed into a mask of fixed, horrified disbelief.

What? thought Chris. *What is it?*

Like a jerky old-fashioned film, the man's limbs began to move and he started to back away. One step back, two, three, his eyes never for a second leaving the source of his fear.

Open-mouthed with astonishment, Chris watched this strange transformation.

Suddenly the man whipped around and began to run back the way he had come, arms and legs flailing frantically. Running, it seemed, for his very life.

At that second Chris became aware of a heavy, musky smell. Before he had time to register this new phenomenon, the ground shook to the thump of heavy feet and there was a sudden rush of air as, from somewhere behind him, a swift, amber form hurled itself past, so close it almost brushed against him.

There was hardly time for Chris to comprehend what was happening before it was all over. Almost in the space of a thought the lion had closed, with great bounding leaps, the gap between it and its frantically running prey. The man tried to get to a tree.

He almost made it. Almost.

He was just reaching up into the lower branches when the lion caught up with him.

He screamed once as he felt the lion's hot breath on his naked back.

Chris closed his eyes to shut out the horror.

The man did not scream again.

Chapter 16

"SO, THAT'S IT, THEN, IS IT?" ASKED HYRAM.

"Yep," said Mike tersely, "that's it. I told you it was a million to one."

They had reached the Seronera road.

"I've done everything you asked. They're gone."

"Can I come down now, bwana?" inquired Bennie, disconsolate and hot on the roof rack.

"Yes."

Even in the village of Nyabogati no one had seen anything of the poachers or even heard anything of them.

"News travels on the wind here," Mike had said. "If these people have heard nothing, then we've no hope."

Bennie climbed gratefully down and stood with the two men gazing out over Serengeti.

"Pity," said the American. "I would have dearly loved to have paid my respects to those guys."

"Me, too," replied Mike, "but it's over. And before you start telling me who's paying for this safari again, I'll tell you what we're doing now."

"So, tell me."

"What we're doing now is we're getting back in the Land Rover, and we're driving straight to Seronera Lodge, where I am going to sit for the rest of the day replacing my depleted strength with a succession of very cold bottles of beer."

"I'll buy a ticket for that," said Hyram.

"Satisfied?" asked Mike.

"No, not satisfied. Resigned. I won't argue anymore. Let's get going."

"OK," said Mike, "thank goodness for that. In the back, Bennie, I'll drive."

They climbed back into the Land Rover. Mike sighed with relief as he eased himself into the driving seat. He reached forward to the ignition key to fire the engine into life.

Such is fate that, if he had turned that key one hundredth, one thousandth of a second earlier, the rattle of the starter motor would have drowned the sound that they all, quite unmistakably, heard.

No one spoke at first. Mike's hand remained poised at the ignition key. He and the American stared straight ahead through the dusty windshield. Bennie, who was still outside the Land Rover, stood motionless.

Finally Hyram broke the silence.

"Bennie," he said.

"Yes, bwana?"

"That twenty dollars."

"Yes, bwana?"

"It's a hundred if you know where that shot came from."

Mike closed his eyes and wearily put his thumb and forefinger to the bridge of his nose.

"Dear God," he said, "I could almost taste that beer."

"It's them," said Hyram quietly, measuredly. "I know it's them. My bones tell me it's them."

"Behind us, bwana. It came from behind us. Over there behind that hill."

Mike started the engine and reversed the vehicle around in a semicircle.

About fifteen miles, he guessed, to the long, low hill that Bennie was pointing toward. At least an hour's drive. Probably more.

"One last try?" pleaded the American meekly.

"One last try," replied Mike, "and I do mean last. Bennie!"

"I know, bwana, I know. On the roof."

"On the roof."

Chapter 17

ALREADY THE VULTURES WERE PACING UP AND DOWN, their wings outstretched, their sharp, ugly heads craning forward, a few feet from the body. They screeched raucously and hideously as they picked up the smell of blood from the almost severed neck.

It is hard to feel anything but revulsion for something so deformed-looking as the grounded vulture. The worst imaginings of a nightmare could hardly conjure something so jerkily grotesque as this mad, hellish creature with its fixed, fanatic eyes, dancing its uncoordinated mad dwarf's dance around the dead.

Yet Chris could not hate even them, so great was his relief.

There was no doubt that the man was dead. In the few seconds after the lion had rushed past him, Chris had kept his eyes closed. He had heard the terrible fleshy thud and the single scream. And he had waited, paralyzed with imagination. Waited for the thump of heavy paws approaching him. Waited for the hot breath as the jaws opened again.

But nothing came.

When he opened his eyes again he was in time to see the last convulsive spasms of the man's limbs be replaced by the unmistakable stillness of death. Almost immediately there was a rush of air as the vultures glided over his head, circled once, and landed on the far side of the body, putting it between them and the lion. Their patience had been rewarded, unexpectedly soon.

The lion had no interest in his kill anyway. The job had been done. The threat had been disposed of.

And now the lion had moved away, squatted on his haunches, and was quietly licking his wound. Chris was close enough to him to be able to see the blood on his teeth. It made him feel nauseous, and he shuddered as he sat, rubbing his twisted ankle. The lion was breathing very heavily, a rapid rasping in his throat. His bony rib cage rose and fell with unnatural speed. Chris thought he could see the animal's heart banging against his ribs.

He had not even glanced at Chris. Made no sign that he even knew he was there, just a few feet from him. Yet Chris knew full well that his presence was not unnoticed. Strangely he felt no fear, no threat from this awesome wild thing near him.

He watched the animal licking his wound.

Two cripples together, he thought wryly.

The sound of the Land Rover rattling into life drew his eyes back to the tree where he had slept. There was a crashing of gears as a gunshot-wounded leg wrestled with the clutch, and then the Land Rover ground into view. Chris held his breath. Injured or not, the remaining man still had the gun. But he was obviously not game to face the lion, gun or not, for the vehicle turned and began to grind slowly away. The lion raised his head and growled a warning as the engine noise began to recede.

Chris looked back at the great, snarling head. He shook his own head in disbelief. Twice this fearful animal had crossed his path. Twice this great creature, this most ferocious of wild spirits, had interceded at a moment of life-threatening danger and delivered him from it. Twice he had been within touching distance of an animal feared above all animals by all living things. And twice he had felt no fear.

From the moment he had left the kopje on his uncertain, dismaying journey, he had known that he was not walking alone. Now he knew what had accompanied him. The animal had been near him all along. Unseen, but somehow subliminally known to be there.

Still it gave no hint that it was aware of the boy's presence. No look, no growl. Nothing.

Chris realized that the pain in his leg was receding

now. Gingerly he stretched it out. He moved very slowly, anxious not to startle the lion. Then he rolled over onto one knee, his hurt leg straight out behind him. With infinite care he stood and put some weight on his ankle. It hurt, but not too much to bear. He took one step on it, successfully. Then another. It supported him. It was all right. He could still walk.

The lion ignored him completely. Chris studied him. He had stopped licking his leg and was sitting back, doglike, presenting a massive, bony profile. And suddenly Chris was so saddened that tears filled his eyes. The animal was so old, he realized, so terribly old. His breath was the rasp of failing lungs, his frame the emerging skeleton of death. Age dripped from the hanging folds of his once-glowing coat, now dull and mangy.

But it was his eyes that riveted Chris's attention. His eyes gazed with such longing, such hope, that they hurt Chris deep into his being. His eyes held the bright shimmer of memory, the luminosity of the old beginning their last, desperately lonely journey. In those eyes was the brief, guttering flare of a dying candle.

Chris turned away. It was too much. Too much to fathom this strange, deeply disturbing presence. Too much to contemplate such greatness grown so old.

Instead his eyes followed the animal's gaze. What was it? What could he see out there that held such promise for him? That transfixed him into such statuesque immobility? But try as he could, Chris could see nothing to account for it. There was nothing but the plain and emptiness—nothing save for that single, long, low hill.

Deeply distressed, he began to limp slowly away from the lion and back toward the tree. Somehow his own uncertainty had gone. Whether he would survive, whether pitting himself against such odds as Africa had thrown at him was insanity, whether he would ever make it to safety, all the doubts that had been gnawing at his confidence, all were suddenly allayed. He felt calm and sure. Only a few miles more to the hill. The hill was safety. He knew it with a certainty such as he had never felt about anything in his life. The hill was the one absolute, emerging like a lifeboat from the mist to the shipwrecked sailor.

He reached the tree. Quietly, methodically, he gathered up the water bottle and food into his bag and swung it onto his back. He draped the shirt around his neck like a scarf and, with calm, unhurried determination, turned to face the final, limping miles.

And he began to walk again.

He did not look back.

He did not need to look back.

He knew.

Two hundred yards behind him the lion had risen to his feet and was walking, too.

Chapter 18

THE GOING HAD BEEN ROUGH, EVEN FOR A LAND ROVER. The ground had been crisscrossed with water courses gouged out by the wet season's swollen streams, some so deep that they had to detour around them. But they had bounced and crashed their way in as straight a line as possible, the occupants thrown about inside, Bennie clinging precariously to the roof in danger of being thrown off onto the ground. Eventually they arrived at the foot of the hill. Then, with the vehicle creeping in low gear up the steep sides, they had halted just below the crest.

Mike grabbed his binoculars, and the three men walked cautiously over the top of the hill until they commanded a panorama of the plain on the other side. Bennie and the American were silent as Mike raised the glasses to his eyes and began to scan methodically around. Pivoting slowly from left to right and back again, he sectioned the land below him, aware that a green Land Rover would be easily missed in a tree shadow or a patch of dark foliage. Hyram held his breath as well as his tongue.

After several minutes Mike spoke.

"Nothing."

"Damn. Goddamn. I was sure . . . ," Hyram hissed. "Look again. They're down there somewhere, I know it. Look at every goddamn tree. They're there."

"You look, if you're so certain."

"I will. Gimme those glasses."

Mike slipped the leather strap over his head and passed them to him. He slumped onto a nearby rock and stared disconsolately out over the plain. He wondered if this pigheaded man would ever give up. His arms ached from battling with the steering wheel. He had a stabbing pain in his back from the constant jolting and banging, and he was very hot, very thirsty, and very fed up. This was it. He'd had enough. In two minutes he was going to put his foot down once and for all and tell this fool of a man that if he didn't get back in the Land Rover and keep his mouth shut until they got to Seronera Lodge, then he'd go without him and leave him here to his fate.

His eyes wandered idly over the plain as he sat with these satisfying thoughts. Below him zebra were grazing quietly under trees, emerging gradually as the sun passed its zenith. Things were beginning to move again after the inactivity of midday. A few herds of gazelle and wildebeest, from this height, looked like dark clouds whispering slowly across the grass. Here and there a warthog scuttled busily.

And then another movement caught his eye. Below, out from the foot of the hill, his experienced eye latched onto a movement that somehow he couldn't put his finger on. Something that wasn't right. Something that didn't fit. He narrowed his eyes. It looked almost like . . .

"Hey," he said, "give me those binoculars, quickly."

"Ha-ha," said the American. "Got something? There you are, I told you. I knew I was right. What is it? What can you see?"

"Will you, for goodness' sake, shut up and give me those glasses," snapped Mike. "There's something over there worries me. And it's not your damned Land Rover, it's something else."

He lay down on the ground and put the glasses up to his eyes again, scanning out to where he had seen the movement.

"There's something there . . . ," he murmured, almost to himself, turning the focusing wheel gradually as he searched.

The glasses stopped moving.

"My God," whispered Mike, stunned.

"What? What is it?" shouted the American.

"Quiet," snapped Mike with a vehemence that silenced the man instantly. "I can't believe what I'm seeing. It's a boy. Dear God, it's a boy down there.

A white boy. What in heaven's name does he think he's doing?"

"There must be a tourist party down there, and he's wandered away from them, do you think?" asked Bennie.

"I can't see anybody else at all," said Mike, carefully scanning the area around the boy. "There's just the boy. Where on earth has he—"

He stopped, abruptly. Too abruptly.

"Bwana?" inquired Bennie, anxiously.

"Bennie." There was a quiet urgency now in Mike's voice. "That child down there. There's a lion behind him. About two hundred yards behind him."

Bennie hissed sharply through his teeth.

Mike spoke again.

"Now do this very quickly and very carefully, Bennie. Go back to the Land Rover and get the rifle. Put two shells in it—don't waste time with any more. If I don't get it with two, I won't get it. Clip the telescopic sight on and be back here in ten seconds with the gun ready to fire."

"Yes, bwana." And he was gone, instantly and silently over the brow of the hill.

Mike swung the binoculars back onto the boy. He appeared to be walking steadily, without hurrying, toward them. He obviously had no idea of the terrible danger he was in. No idea that he was being stalked by the most dangerous beast of all. The animal, too, was walking steadily and determinedly after the boy, his head down, following his scent.

"Hurry, Bennie, damn you, hurry."

Mike's hands began to shake a little. What was facing him was the worst situation any hunter has to face. He has in reality only one shot, and that shot must kill, or at very least immobilize. An injured animal becomes a greater danger than before and will kill in a frenzy of pain and vengeance. Mike knew that if the first bullet didn't bring the animal down there would be no second. And the life of that small boy down there would be quickly and bloodily brought to a close. The lion would connect the injury with his prey and wreak revenge.

Mike felt himself beginning to sweat and wiped his hand across his brow.

Bennie slumped beside him, the rifle in his hands.

"Loaded ready, bwana. Safety catch off."

"Right," said Mike. "Get the binoculars and get your eyes on that lion. I want to know exactly where I hit him. If I don't drop him, make sure you keep sight of him."

"Yes, bwana. Good luck, bwana."

"Have you got him in sight?"

"Got him, bwana."

Mike wiped his palms on his shirt, then put the rifle up to his shoulder. He brought up the barrel and peered into the telescopic sight, moving the rifle from side to side slowly, trying to locate the beast.

"Got him," he said, as the figure slid into the sight.

"Now," he said, "one shot. One shot only. Straight in the heart."

With infinite care he tracked the center of the hairline cross back from the lion's head, past the shoulder, to the rib cage.

"That's it. Now, slowly does it. Neat and clean."

His hands had steadied now the moment was upon him. He concentrated every cell of his mind upon keeping the rifle steady, the cross centered precisely on the lion's heart.

Suddenly the lion stopped and stood stock-still, his head hanging low.

Perfect, thought Mike. *What a stroke of luck. A perfect target.*

And slowly, imperceptibly, his finger began to apply a gentle, progressive, fatal pressure on the trigger.

Chapter 19

THERE WAS NO SUDDEN FLASH OF REALIZATION. CHRIS could not even put his finger on the moment he knew. It had been so gradual, so natural, that it seemed as if he had known all along. As if there had never been any alternative, never any need for fear, or worry, or wonder. It was not even something to question. Too much had happened in these last days for anything to be a surprise or to require an explanation. It was simply happening, and Chris accepted that it was happening, gratefully, and without feeling any need to ask why. For their different reasons they were both going to the same place. They were traveling together.

Together, yet not together.

No visible signs passed from one to the other. No looks, no sounds. The gap between them never got less than two hundred yards. But nor did it ever get more. When the boy stopped to rest, the lion stopped, too. When the lion stopped, the boy would know it and would wait quietly for him to gather his strength again.

So, together yet apart, they moved toward the hill, each pulled by his own sure guiding thread.

In the last miles Chris gained in strength as the lion weakened. As the beast's head hung lower and his progress became more painful, so the boy's head rose higher and the pain in his ankle dissipated. It was as though he was feeding from the animal's ebbing spirit, drawing energy from the last glowing embers of his slow determination. But the embers were fading quickly. The lion needed to rest more and more frequently. Every few hundred yards he would simply stop walking and stand motionless, his head so low that his soft muzzle almost touched the ground. And there he would remain for several minutes, like a high-altitude climber sucking precious oxygen from desperately thin air, before lurching into motion again to tackle the next few yards of his lonely ascent. He would neither sit nor lie to take his rest, as though should he lie he would never rise again.

Sometimes Chris could not even see him when he turned and looked. But he always knew where he was, always knew when he stopped, always knew when the moment came to move again. He tried to feed some of his strength back to the lion, willing him as he had before, back at the kopje, to live. As the realization of where the beast was going, and why, permeated him, his sadness for the age and failing powers of the creature had changed into a natural resignation. The vague, mystic feeling he had had earlier, in that disturbing second when their eyes had met, was resolved. Somehow, at that moment, in the great unexplained and unexplainable universe of the mind, a nerve had been touched in both of them. A tied knot had been recognized. In their separate distress they had found a mutual dependency. A shared need. Neither would succeed without the other. Both knew the truth of this. And both now carried in their hearts the knowledge that they would succeed, and that their success would give life to one and take it from the other.

The lion sank to the ground and laid his great head on his outstretched paws. It seemed to him now that darkness was falling, though his senses told him that it was not yet that part of the day. Things were blurred at the edges of his vision, and movements there dismayed him by their imperceptibility. Though the afternoon sun still flared in an incandescent sky, dusk was closing around and within him. He had no pain now. His body felt warm and comfortable, though strangely distant. And everywhere was so quiet. So quiet it gave him unease. He had never known such quiet. He could no longer see the hill; it was swallowed by twilight. It didn't matter. He knew where he was with a certainty that had no need of sight. He was almost there.

Just a short rest, and the strength would come for him to finish.

He closed his eyes.

Chris felt him stop and stopped, too, as he had so many times in the past hours. He waited. But this time the feeling was different, and he knew immediately that the lion's life was slipping away from him with his journey not yet completed. He could not allow this to happen. If he were to leave him lying there, somehow his own journey would not be complete either, even though he was sure now of his success. Perhaps there was no help that he could give. But he had to try.

Without hesitation he turned and started to walk back to him, unaware that from the hill three astonished pairs of eyes were watching him. Unaware that this simple act, which seemed to him so natural, so inevitable, had stopped a bullet winging down from the hilltop.

To the end of his days Mike Taylor would marvel that he was unable to pull that trigger. He rationalized that, out of the corner of his eye, he had seen the boy turn, and that this had distracted him. This, anyway, was what he told those who questioned him. But he knew himself that it was not true.

Whatever the reason, he lowered the gun, unfired, and laid it to one side.

Perhaps it was the certainty with which the boy turned, the calmness and sureness with which he walked, that captured the minds of the three men on the hill and held them silent. Privileged watchers, enrapt witnesses to wonder, they felt, all three the same, a "rightness" about what they saw that allayed all fear for the boy. Rather they felt an inexplicable awe as they saw the boy approach the lion, for long minutes stand motionless a few feet away from him, then turn his back and begin to walk away again. And with a deep wonderment that was to remain with them forever, they watched the lion rise shakily to his feet and, with slow, careful steps, begin to follow the boy.

So, together, they passed the last mile, strange companions in a stranger journey.

Long before they reached the foot of the hill Chris could see the men just below the crest. There was no great flood of relief. Satisfaction, rather, that he had been right. He had known that help would be here. There was no temptation to run to them, and he was glad to see that they made no move to descend to meet him. He did not want anything to deflect the old animal from its path now.

They rose together up the side of the hill, the boy first, the great, slow figure, like a huge, faithful, golden dog, a few feet behind. Two spirits caught and held. Bound in a magic, brief but eternal.

And suddenly the thread began to break.

Though darkness had drowned his eyes, the lion began to feel things beneath his feet, in the very fabric of the ground, that he knew. Things long past but stored, deep in the mind, began to whir into his consciousness. Long-forgotten shapes flitted in shadow-play in his twilit eyes, and on the air the clear, silver music of memory called.

He turned toward it.

He was home.

Their journey ended, they took their separate ways. Chris did not stop. There was no need. The spell was broken. Each was free. So Chris simply kept on walking.

But, as he rose up the final feet to safety, there was a knowledge within him deeper than mind could define, deeper still than emotion could process. As the great beast turned away, and the boy's feet took him upward, the thread that had held them in this brief, magical thrall tautened, stretched and tensed, until it tore away.

And as it tore it took a small piece of both their hearts.

Epilogue

IN THE YEARS TO COME, AS THE STORY WAS TOLD AGAIN and again in the bars of Nairobi, embroidered by those who draw stature from the sensational, or diminished by those whose eyes are curtained by logic, the cynics held the day.

"The boy was lucky," they said. "The lion was dying. He didn't even know the boy was there. The lad probably imagined it all. He'd had a blow on the head, hadn't he? There you are, then. He was delirious. In shock. If he'd ever got near that lion it would have bitten him in half."

And, with the unshakable confidence of ignorance, they parceled up the story, labeled it "fantasy" and shelved it under "fairy tale."

But they had not been there. They had not seen.

A year later, to the day, those who had lived this story gathered on that lonely hilltop, in a still Serengeti afternoon, to remember. Mike and Bennie; the pilot and his family; even Hyram Johnson had flown back especially to stand with Chris and his father, here, on this day. The thanks had long ago been said, the bodies healed, the lives returned to normal. Or as normal as those touched by these events could be.

Chris was taller and broader now. He bore no scars, mental or physical, from those terrible days. The only legacy was carried in his eyes. Those who looked into them would see a pensive, farsighted gaze, fixed on something at a great distance; something invisible but very sad. The same look as in Mike Taylor's eyes. Eyes that have seen into Africa and come to terms with its savagery and nobility.

"Was that where he went?" Chris asked Mike.

"Yes. He cut across there and disappeared between those rocks. Do you want to go down?"

"No. I just wanted to know. Was he ever seen again?"

"No. I shouldn't think he ever came out again. He'd found what he wanted."

They sat looking down the hillside, quietly remembering.

"What was it, do you think? What made him come with me?"

"I don't know," said Mike, gently. "He was dying.

That's the loneliest journey anyone can take. I think
perhaps he just needed a bit of company. We all need
a friend."

"Ach," snorted Bennie, contemptuously. "That's
wazungu talk."

"I beg your pardon," said Mike, huffily.

Chris grinned. "Come on, Bennie. What do you
say?"

"This place," said Bennie. "Do you know what it's
called?"

"Soit Naado Murt," replied Mike. "The Long-
necked Stone."

"Yes," said Bennie. "That's what the maps say. But
the Masai have a nickname for it. Simba Rocks. The
Place of Lions."

He smiled affectionately at Chris.

"The Masai tell your story in the *bomas* now,
bwana Chris. They know why the simba came with
you."

"Why?"

"Because, they say, the lion looked at you and saw
a heart as brave as his own. That's why."

Glossary
(Kiswahili Words)

boma   a village or settlement, usually thorn fenced
bwana   mister/sir
Chagga   East African tribe
fundi   mechanic/handyman
kopje (pronounced "copy")   a low rocky outcrop, frequently the home of lions
Masai   East African tribe
mzee (pronounced "um-zay") respected elder gentleman
mzungu   white man
simba   lion
tembo   elephant
wazungu   whites